ANDREW THE GLAD

MARIA THOMPSON DAVIESS

1st WORLD
LIBRARY
Literary Society

Andrew the Glad

Maria Thompson Daviess

© 1st World Library, 2006
PO Box 2211
Fairfield, IA 52556
www.1stworldlibrary.com
First Edition

LCCN: 2006936223

Softcover ISBN: 978-1-4218-3087-2
Hardcover ISBN: 978-1-4218-2987-6
eBook ISBN: 978-1-4218-3187-9

Purchase *"Andrew the Glad"*
as a traditional bound book at:
www.1stWorldLibrary.com/purchase.asp?ISBN=978-1-4218-3087-2

1st World Library is a literary, educational organization dedicated to:

- Creating a free internet library of downloadable ebooks

- Hosting writing competitions and offering book publishing scholarships.

Interested in more 1st World Library books?
contact: literacy@1stworldlibrary.com
Check us out at: www.1stworldlibrary.com

1st World Library Literary Society

Giving Back to the World

"If you want to work on the core problem, it's early school literacy."

- James Barksdale, former CEO of Netscape

"No skill is more crucial to the future of a child, or to a democratic and prosperous society, than literacy."

- Los Angeles Times

Literacy... means far more than learning how to read and write... The aim is to transmit... knowledge and promote social participation."

- UNESCO

"Literacy is not a luxury, it is a right and a responsibility. If our world is to meet the challenges of the twenty-first century we must harness the energy and creativity of all our citizens."

- President Bill Clinton

"Parents should be encouraged to read to their children, and teachers should be equipped with all available techniques for teaching literacy, so the varying needs and capacities of individual kids can be taken into account."

- Hugh Mackay

TO LIBBIE LUTTRELL MORROW

CONTENTS

CHAPTER I

THE HEART TRAP

"There are some women who will brew mystery from the decoction of even a very simple life. Matilda is one of them," remarked the major to himself as he filled his pipe and settled himself before his high-piled, violet-flamed logs. "It was waxing strong in her this morning and an excitement will arrive shortly. Now I wonder—"

"Howdy, Major," came in a mockingly lugubrious voice from the hall, and David Kildare blew into the room. He looked disappointedly around, dropped into a chair and lowered his voice another note.

"Seen Phoebe?" he demanded.

"No, haven't you?" answered the major as he lighted his pipe and regarded the man opposite him with a large smile of welcome.

"Not for three days, hand-running. She's been over to see Andy with Mrs. Matilda twice, and I've missed her both times. Now, how's that for luck?"

"Well," said the major reflectively, "in the terms of modern parlance, you certainly are up against it. And did it ever occur to you that a man with three ribs broken and a dislocated collar-bone, who has written a play and a sprinkle of poems, is likely to interest Phoebe Donelson enormously? There is nothing like poetry to implant a divine passion, and Andrew is undoubtedly of poetic stamp."

"Oh, poetry—hang! It's more Andy's three ribs than anything else. He just looks pale and smiles at all of 'em. He always did have yellow dog eyes, the sad kind. I'd like to smash all two dozen of his ribs," and Kildare slashed at his own sturdy legs with his crop. He had dropped in with his usual morning's tale of woe to confide to Major Buchanan, and he had found him, as always, ready to hand out an incendiary brand of sympathy.

"He ought not to have more than twenty-three; one on the right side should be missing. Some woman's got it—maybe Phoebe," said the major with deadly intent.

"Nothing of the kind. I'm shy a rib myself and Phoebe is *it.* Don't I get a pain in my side every time I see her? It's the real psychic thing, only she doesn't seem to get hold of her end of the wire like she might."

"Don't trust her, David, don't trust her! You see his being injured in Panama, building bridges for his country, while you sat here idly reading the newspapers about it, has had its appeal. I know it's dangerous, but you ought to want Phoebe to soothe his fevered brow. Nothing is too good for a hero this side of Mason and Dixon's, my son." The major eyed his victim with calculating coolness, gaging just how much more of the baiting he would stand. He was disappointed to see that the train of explosives he had laid failed to take fire.

"Well, he's being handed out a choice bunch of Mason-Dixon attentions. They are giving him the cheer-up all day long. When I left, Mrs. Shelby was up there talking to him, and Mrs. Cherry Lawrence and Tom had just come in. Mrs. Cherry had brought him several fresh eggs. She had got them from Phoebe! I sent them to her from the farm this morning. Rode out and coaxed the hens for them myself. Now, isn't a brainstorm up to me?"

"Well, I don't know," answered the major in a judicial tone of voice. "You wouldn't have them neglect him, would you?"

"Well, what about me?" demanded David dolefully. "I haven't any green eyes, 'cause I'm trusting Andy, *not* Phoebe; but neglect is just withering my leaves. I haven't seen her alone for two weeks. She is always over there with Mrs. Matilda and the rest 'soothing the fevered brow.' Say, Major, give Mrs. Matilda the hint. The chump isn't really sick any more. Hint that a little less—"

"David, sir," interrupted the major, "it takes more than a hint to stop a woman when she takes a notion to nurse an attractive man, a sick lion one at that. And depend upon it, it is the poetry that makes them hover him, not the ribs."

"Well, you just stop her and that'll stop them," said David wrathfully.

"David Kildare," answered the major dryly, "I've been married to her nearly forty years and I've never stopped her doing anything yet. Stopping a wife is one of the bride-notions a man had better give up early in the matrimonial state—if he expects to hold the bride. And bride-holding ought to be the life-job of a man who is rash enough to undertake one."

"Do you think Phoebe and bride will ever rhyme together, Major?" asked David in a tone of deepest depression. "I can't seem to hear them ever jingle."

"Yes, Dave, the Almighty will meter it out to her some day, and I hope He will help you when He does. I can't manage my wife. She's a modern woman. Now, what are we going to do about them?" and the major smiled quizzically at the perturbed young man standing on the rug in front of the fire.

"Well," answered Kildare with a spark in his eyes, as he flecked a bit of mud from his boots which were splashed from his morning ride, "when I get Phoebe Donelson, I'm going to whip her!" And very broad and tall and strong was young David but not in the least formidable as to expression.

"Dave, my boy," answered the major in a tone of the deepest respect, "I hope you will do it, if you get the chance; but you won't! Thirty-eight years ago last summer I felt the same way, but I've had a long time to make up my mind to it; and I haven't done it yet."

"Anyway," rejoined his victim, "there's just this to it; she has got to accept me kindly, affectionately and in a ladylike manner or I'm going to be the villain and make some sort of a rough house to frighten her into it."

"David," said the major with emphasis, "don't count on frightening a woman into a compliance in an affair of the affections. Don't you know they will risk having their hearts suspended on a hair-line between heaven and hell and enjoy it? Now, my wife—"

"Oh, Mrs. Matilda never could have been like that," interrupted David miserably.

"Boy," answered the major solemnly, "if I were to give you a succinct account of the writhings of my soul one summer over a California man, the agony you are enduring would seem the extremity of insignificance."

"Heavenly hope, Major, did you have to go up against the other man game, too? I seem to have been standing by with a basket picking up chips of Phoebe's lovers for a long lifetime; Tom, Hob, Payt, widowers and flocks of new fledges. But I had an idea that you must have been a first-and-only with Mrs. Matilda."

"Well, it sometimes happens, David, that the individuality of all of a woman's first loves get so merged into that of the last that it would be difficult for her to differentiate them herself; and it is best to keep her happily employed so she doesn't try."

"Well, all I can say for you, Major," interrupted Kildare with a laugh, "is that your forty years' work shows some. Your Mrs. Buchanan is what I call a finished product of a wife. I'll never do it in the world. I can get up and talk a jury into seeing things my way, but I get cross-brained when I go to put things to Phoebe. That reminds me, that case on old Jim Cross for getting tangled up with some fussy hens in Latimer's hen-house week before last is called for to-day at twelve sharp. I'm due to put the old body through and pay the fine and costs; only the third time this year. I'm thinking of buying him a hen farm to save myself trouble. Good-by, sir!"

"David, David," laughed the major, "beware of your growing responsibilities! Cap Hobson reported that sensation of yours before the grand jury over that negro and policeman trouble. The darkies will put up your portrait beside that of Father Abe on Emancipation Day and you will be in danger of passing down to posterity by the public-spirit-fame chute. Your record will be in the annals of the city if you don't mind!"

"Not much danger, Major," answered David with a smile. "I'm just a glad man with not balance enough to run the rail of any kind of heavy track affairs."

"David," said the major with a sudden sadness coming into his voice and eyes, "one of the greatest men I ever knew we called the glad man—the boy's father, Andrew Sevier. We called him Andrew, the Glad. Something has brought it all back to me to-day and with your laugh you reminded me of him. The tragedy of it all!"

"I've always known what a sorrow it was to you, Major, and it is the bitterness that is eating the heart out of Andy. What was it all about exactly, sir? I have always wanted to ask you." David looked into the major's stern old eyes with such a depth of sympathy in his young ones that a barrier suddenly melted and with the tone of bestowing an honor the old fire-eater told the tale of the sorrow of his youth.

"Gaming was in his blood, David, and we all knew it and protected him from high play always. We were impoverished gentlemen, who were building fences and restoring war-devastated lands, and we played in our shabby club with a minimum stake and a maximum zest for the sport. But that night we had no control over him. He had been playing in secret with Peters Brown for weeks and had lost heavily. When we had closed up the game, he called for the dice and challenged Brown to square their account. They threw again and again with luck on the same grim side. I saw him stake first his horses, then his bank account, and lose.

"Hayes Donelson and I started to remonstrate but he silenced us with a look. Then he drew a hurried transference of his Upper Cumberland property and put it on the table. They threw again and he lost! Then he smiled and with a steady hand wrote a conveyance of his home and plantation, the last things he had, as we knew, and laid that on the table."

"No, Major," exclaimed David with positive horror in his voice.

"Yes, it was madness, boy," answered the major. "Brown turned his ivories and we all held our breath as we read his four-three. A mad joy flamed in Andrew's face and he turned his cup with a steady wrist—and rolled threes. We none of us looked at Brown, a man who had led another man in whose veins ran a madness, where in his ran ice, on to his ruin. We followed Andrew to the street to see him ride away in a gray drizzle to a gambled home—and a wife and son.

"That morning deeds were drawn, signed, witnessed and delivered to Brown in his office. Then—then"—the major's thin, powerful old hands grasped the arm of his chair—"we found him in the twilight under the clump of cedars that crowned the hill which overlooked Deep-mead Farm—broad acres of land that the Seviers had had granted them from Virginia—*dead*, his pistol under his shoulder and a smile on his face. Just so he had looked as he rode at the head of our crack gray regiment in that hell-reeking charge at Perryville, and it was such a smile we had followed into the trenches at Franklin. Stalwart, dashing, joyous Andrew, how we had all loved him, our man-of-smiles!"

"Can anything ever make it up to you, Major?" asked David softly. As he spoke he refilled the major's pipe and handed it to him, not appearing to notice how the lean old hand shook.

"You do, sir," answered the major with a spark coming back into his eyes, "you and your gladness and the boy and his—sadness—and Phoebe most of all. But don't let me keep you from your hen-roost defense—I agree with you that a hen farm will be the cheapest course for you to take with old Cross. Give him my respects, and good-by to you." The major's dismissal was gallant, and David went his way with sympathy and admiration in his gay heart for the old fire-eater whose ashes had been so stirred.

The major resumed his contemplation of the fire. Hearty burning logs make good companions for a philosopher like the major, and such times when his depths were troubled he was wont to trust to them for companionship.

But into any mood of absorption, no matter how deep, the major was always ready to welcome Mrs. Matilda, and his expectations on the subject of her adventures had been fully realized. As usual she had begun her tale in the exact center of the adventure with full liberty left herself to work back to the beginning or forward to the close.

"And the mystery of it all, Matilda, is the mystery of love—warm, contradictory, cruel, human love that the Almighty puts in the heart of a man to draw the unreasoning heart of a woman; sometimes to bruise and crush it, seldom to kill it outright. Mary Caroline only followed her call," answered the major, responding to her random lead patiently.

"I know, Major; yes, I know," answered his wife as she laid her hand on the arm of his chair. "Mary Caroline struggled against it but it was stronger than she was. It wasn't the loving and marrying a man who had been on the other side—so many girls did marry Union officers as soon as they could come back down to get them—but the *kind* of enemy he was!"

"Yes," said the major thoughtfully, "it would take a wider garment of love to cover a man with a carpetbag in his hand than a soldier in a Yankee uniform. A conqueror who looked around as he was fighting and then came back to trade on the necessities of the conquered cuts but a sorry figure, Matilda, but a sorry figure!"

"And Mary Caroline felt it too, Major—but she couldn't help it," said Mrs. Buchanan with a catch in her voice. "The night before she ran away to marry him she spent with me, for you were away across the river, and all night we talked. She told me—not that she was going—but how she cared. She said it bitterly over and over, 'Peters Brown, the carpetbagger—and I love him!' I tried to comfort her as best I could but it was useless. He was a thief to steal her—just a child!" There was a bitterness and contempt in Mrs. Matilda's usually tender voice. She sat up very straight and there was a sparkle in her bright eyes.

"And the girl," continued the major thoughtfully, "was born as her mother died. He'd never let the mother come back and he never brought the child. Now he's dead. I wonder—I wonder. We've got a claim on that girl, Matilda. We—"

"And, dear, that is just what I came back in such a hurry to tell you about—I felt it so—I haven't been able to say it right away. I began by talking about Mary Caroline and—I—I—"

"Why, Matilda!" said the major in vague alarm at the tremble in his wife's voice. He laid his hand over hers on the arm of his chair with a warm clasp.

"It's just this, Major. You know how happy I have been, we all

Maria Thompson Daviess

have been, over the wonderful statue that has been given in memory of the women of the Confederacy who stayed at home and fed the children and slaves while the men fought. As you advised them, they have decided to put it in the park just to the left of the Temple of Arts, on the very spot where General Darrah had his last gun fired and spiked just before he fell and just as the surrender came. It's strange, isn't it, that nobody knows who's giving it? Perhaps it was because you and David and I were talking last night about what he should say about General Darrah when he made the presentation of the sketches of the statue out at the opening of the art exhibition in the Temple of Arts to-night, that made me dream about Mary Caroline all night. It is all so strange." Again Mrs. Buchanan paused with a half sob in her voice.

"Why, what is it, Matilda?" the major asked as he turned and looked at her anxiously.

"It's a wonderful thing that has happened, Major. Something, I don't know what, just made me go out to the Temple this morning to see the sketches of the statue which came yesterday. I felt I couldn't wait until to-night to see them. Oh, they are so lovely! Just a tall fearless woman with a baby on her breast and a slave woman clinging to her skirts with her own child in her arms!

"As I stood before the case and looked at them the tragedy of all the long fight came back to me. I caught my breath and turned away—and there stood a girl! I knew her instantly, for I was looking straight into Mary Caroline's own purple eyes. Then I just opened my arms and held her close, calling Mary Caroline's name over and over. There was no one else in the great room and it was quiet and solemn and still. Then she put her hand against my face and looked at me and said in the loveliest tenderest voice:

"'It's my mother's Matilda, isn't it? I have the old daguerreotype!' And I smiled back and we kissed each other and cried—and then cried some more."

"I haven't a doubt of those tears," answered the major in a suspiciously gruff voice. "But where's the girl? Why didn't you bring her right back with you? She is ours, Matilda, that purple-eyed girl. When is she coming? Call Tempie and tell her to have Jane get those two south-wing rooms ready right away. I want Jeff to fill up the decanters with the fifty-six claret, too, and to put—"

"But wait, Major, I couldn't get her to come home with me! We went out into the sunshine and for a long drive into the country. We talked and talked. It is the saddest thing in the world, but she is convinced that her mother's people are not going to like her. She has been taught that we are so prejudiced. I think she has found out about the carpetbagging. She is so sensitive! She came because she couldn't help it; she wanted just to see her mother's country. She's only been here two days. She intends to steal away back now, over to Europe, I think. I tried to make her see—"

"Matilda," said the major sternly, "go right back and tell that child to pack her dimity and come straight here to me. Carpetbagging, indeed!—Mary Caroline's girl with purple eyes! Did old Brown have any purple eyes, I'd like to know?"

"I made her promise not to go until tomorrow. I think she would feel differently if we could get her to stay a little while. I want her to stay. She is so lonely. My little boy loved Mary Caroline and grieved for her when she went away. I feel I must have this child to comfort for a time at least."

"Of course she must stay. Did she promise she wouldn't slip away from you?"

"Yes, but I'm uneasy. I think I will go down to her hotel right now. Do you mind about being alone for lunch? Does Tempie get your coffee right?"

"She does pretty well considering that she hasn't been tasting it for thirty years. But you go get that child, Matilda. Bring her

Maria Thompson Daviess

right back with you. Don't stop to argue with her, I'll attend to all that later; just bring her home!"

And as Mrs. Buchanan departed the major rose and stood at the window until he saw her get into her carriage and be driven out of sight. Looking down the vista of the long street, his eyes had a faraway tender light, and as he turned and took up his pipe from the table his thoughts slipped back into the province of memory. He settled himself in his chair before his fire to muse a bit between the whiffs of his heart-leaf.

And Mary Caroline Darrah's girl had come home—home to her own, he mused. There was mystery in it, the mystery that sometimes brands the unborn. Brown had never let Mary Caroline come back and the few letters she had written had told them little of the life she led. The constraint had wrung his wife's yearning heart. Only a letter had come when somehow the news had reached her of the death of Matilda's boy, and it had been wild and sweet and athrob with her love of them. And in its pages her own hopes for the spring were confessed in a passion of desire to give and claim sympathy. Her baby had been born and she was dead and buried before they had heard of it; twenty-three years ago! And Matilda's grief for her own child had been always mingled with love and longing for the motherless, unattainable young thing across the distance. Brown had kept the girl to himself and had never brought her back—because he *dared* not.

The major's powerful old hands writhed around the arms of his chair and his eyes glowed into the embers like live sparks. It was years, nearly thirty years ago—but, God, how the tragedy of it came back! The hot blood beat into his veins and he could feel it and see it all. Would the picture always burn in his brain? Nearly thirty years ago—

The logs crashed apart in the hearth and with a start the major rose to his feet, a tear dashed aside under his shaggy old eyebrows. He would go back to his Immortals—and forget. Perhaps Phoebe would come in for lunch. That would make forgetting easier.

Where had the girl been for the last few days? He smiled as he found himself in something of David's dismay at not having seen the busy young woman for quite a time.

And it was perhaps an hour later that, as he sat in the breakfast room partaking of his lunch in solitary comfort, lost to the world, his wish for her brought its materialization. He had the morning's paper propped up before him and an outspread book rested by his plate, while he held a large volume balanced on his knee, which he paused occasionally to consult.

Mrs. Buchanan had telephoned that she would be home with her guest at five o'clock and his mind was filled with pleasant anticipation. But there was never a time with the major, no matter how filled the life was around him with the excitement of events, with the echo of joy or woe, the clash of social strife or the turmoil of vaster interests, when he failed to be able to plunge into his books and lose himself completely.

He was in the act of consuming a remnant of a corn muffin and a draft from his paper at the same time, when he heard a merry voice in laughing greeting to Jeff, and the rose damask curtains that hung between the breakfast room and the hall parted, and Phoebe stood framed against their heavy folds. She was the freshest, most radiant, tailor-made vision imaginable and the major smiled a large joyful smile at the sight of her.

"Come in, come in, my dear; you are just in time for a hot muffin and a fried chicken wing!" he exclaimed as he rose and drew her to the table. The old volume crashed to the floor unheeded.

"Oh, no, Major, thank you, I couldn't think of it," exclaimed Phoebe. "I'm lunching on a glass of malted milk and a raw egg these days. I lost a pound and three-quarters last week and I feel so slim and graceful." As she spoke she ran her hands down the charming lines of her tall figure and turned slowly

Maria Thompson Daviess

around for him to get the full effect of her loss. She was most beautifully set up and the long lines melted into curves where gracious curves ought to be.

"Nonsense, nonsense, Phoebe Donelson!" exclaimed the major. "Every pound is an added charm. Sit here beside me." And he drew her into a chair at the corner of the table.

In a twinkling of her black eyes Tempie had served her with the golden muffins and crisp chicken. With a long sigh of absolute rapture Phoebe resigned herself to the inevitable crash of her resolutions.

"Ah, I never was so miserable and so happy in all my life before," she said. "I'm so hungry—and I'm so stout—and these muffins are wickedly delicious."

"Phoebe," said the major sternly, "instead of starving yourself to death you need to lie awake at night with lovers' troubles. Why, the summer I courted Matilda I could have wrapped my belt around me twice. I have never been portly since. It's loving you need, good, hard, miserable loving. Didn't you ever hear of a 'lean and hungry lover'? Your conduct is positively— have another muffin and this little slice of upper joint—I say positively, unwomanly inhuman. Are there no depths of pity in your breast? Is your bosom of adamant? When did you see David Kildare? He is in a most pitiable condition. He left here not an hour ago and I felt—"

"Don't worry over David, please, Major," said Phoebe as she paused with a bit of buttered muffin suspended on the way to her white teeth. "He is the most riotously—thank you, Tempie, just one more—happy individual I know. What he wants he has, and he sees to it that he has what he wants—to which add a most glorious leisure in which to want and have."

"Phoebe, David Kildare has an aching void in his heart that weighs just one hundred and thirty-six pounds, lacking now I believe one and three-quarters pounds plus three muffins and a half chicken. How can you be so heartless?" The major bent a benignly stern glance upon her which she returned with the utmost unconcern.

"He did not see you all of yesterday or the day before and only once on Monday, and then you—"

"That sounds like one of those rhyming calendars, my dear Major.

> "Monday I am going far away,
> Tuesday I'll be busy all the day,
> Wednesday is the day I study French,
> Thursday is the—"

and Phoebe hummed the little nonsense jingle to him in a most beguiling manner.

The major laughed delightedly. "Phoebe, some day you will be held responsible for David Kildare's—"

"But, my dear Major," interrupted Phoebe, "how could I be expected to work all day for raiment and food, with malted milk and eggs at the price they are now, and then be responsible for such a perfectly irresponsible person as David Kildare? Why, just yesterday, while I was writing up the Farrell débutante tea with the devil waiting at my elbows for copy and the composing room in a stew, he called me twice over the wire. He knew better, but didn't care."

"Still, my dear, still it's love," said the major as he looked at her thoughtfully and dropped the banter that had been in his voice since she had come in. "A boy's? Perhaps, but I think not. You'll see! It's a call, a call that must be answered some time, child—and a mystery." For a moment the major sat and looked deep into the gray eyes raised to his in quick responsiveness to the change in his mood. "Don't trifle with love, girl, it's God Almighty's dower to a woman. It's hers; though she pays a bitter price for it. It's a wonder and a worker of wonders. It has all come home to me to-day and I think you will understand when I tell you about—"

"Major," interrupted Tempie with a broad grin on her black face, "Mr. Dave, he done telephoned fer you ter keep Miss Phoebe till he gits here. He says he'll hold you and me 'sponsible, sir."

A quick flush rose to Phoebe's cheeks and she laughed as she collected her notebook and pinned down her veil all at the same tune with a view to instant flight. She gave neither the major nor Tempie time for remonstrance.

"Good-by!" she called from the hall. "I only came in to tell Mrs. Matilda that I would meet her at the Cantrell tea at five-fifteen and afterward we could make that visit together. The muffins were divine!"

"Tempie," remarked the major as he looked up at her over the devastated table with an imperturbable smile, "I have decided positively that women are just half-breed angels with devil markings all over their dispositions."

And having received which admonition with the deepest respect, Tempie immediately fell into a perfect whirlwind of guest preparations which involved the pompous Jefferson, her husband, and the meek Jane, her daughter. The major issued her numberless, perfectly impossible but solicitous orders and then retired to his library chair with his mind at ease and his books at hand.

And it was in the violet flamed dusk as he sat with his immortal friends ranged around that Mrs. Matilda brought the treasure home to him. She was a very lovely thing, a fragrant flower of a woman with the tender shyness of a child in her manner as she laid her hands in his outheld to her with his courtly old-world grace.

"My dear, my dear," he said as he drew her near to him,

"here's a welcome that's been ready for you twenty years, you slip of a girl you, with your mother's eyes. Did you think you could get away from Matilda and me when we've been waiting for you all this time?"

"I may have thought so, but when I saw her I knew I couldn't; didn't want to even," she answered him in a low voice that hinted of close-lying tears.

"Child, Matilda has had a heart trap ready for you ever since you were born, in case she sighted you in the open. It's baited with a silver rattle, doll babies, sugar plums, the ashes of twenty years' roses, the fragrance of every violet she has seen, and lately an aggregation of every eligible masculine heart in this part of the country has been added. She caught you fair— walk in and help yourself; it's all yours!"

CHAPTER II

THE RITUAL

"Well, it's a sensation all right, Major," said David as he stood in front of the major's fire early in the morning after the ceremonies of the presentation of sketches of the statue out at the Temple of Arts. "Mrs. Matilda told me the news and helped me sandwich it into my speech between that time and the open-up talk. People had asked so often who was giving the statue, laid it on so many different people, and wondered over it to such an extent all fall that they had got tired and forgot that they didn't know all about it. When I presented it in the name of Caroline Darrah Brown in memory of her mother and her grandfather, General Darrah, you could have heard a pin drop for a few seconds, then the applause was almost a sob. It was as dramatic a thing as has been handed this town in many a day. Still it was a bit sky-rockety, don't you think—keeping it like that and—"

"David," interrupted the major quickly, "she never intended to tell it. She had done the business part of it through her solicitors. She *never* wanted us to know. I persuaded her to let it be presented in her name, myself, just before Matilda went out with you. She shrinks—"

"Wait a minute, Major, don't get the two sides of my brain crossed. You persuaded her—she isn't in town is she?—don't tell me she's here herself!" And David ruffled his auburn forelock with a gesture of perplexity.

"Yes," answered the major, "Caroline Darrah Brown is here and is, I hope, going to stay for a time at least. I wanted to tell you about it yesterday but I hadn't seen her and I—"

"And, David dear," interrupted Mrs. Buchanan who had been standing by with shining eyes waiting for an opening to break in on Kildare's astonishment with some of the details of her happiness over her discovery. "I didn't tell you last night for the major didn't want me to, but she *is* so lovely! She's your inherited friend, for your mother and hers were devoted to each other. I do want you to love her and everybody help me to make her feel at home. Don't mind about her father being a—you know a—a carpetbagger. Three of her Darrah grandfathers have been governors of this state; just think about them and don't talk about her father or any carpet—you know. Please be good to her!"

"Be good to her," exclaimed David heartily, "just watch me! I am loving her already for making you so happy by this down-from-the-sky drop, Mrs. Matilda. And we'll all be careful about the carpetbags; won't even mention a rug; lots of talk can be got out of the dead governors I'm thinking. My welcome's getting more enthusiastic every moment. When can I hand it to her?"

"She's resting now and I think she ought to be quiet for to-day, because she has been under a strain," answered Mrs. Buchanan as she glanced tenderly at a closed door across the hall. "Oh, I'm so glad you think you are going to love her in spite of—of—"

"The Brown graft on the Darrah family tree?" finished David quizzically. His eyes danced with delighted amusement across her puffs at the major as he added, "Must have been silversmiths dangling on most of his ancestral branches, judging from his propensity for making dollars; a million or two, stocks, bonds, any kind of flimflam,—eh, Major?"

"Yes," answered the major as he blew a ring of smoke into the

Maria Thompson Daviess

air, "yes, just about that; any kind of flimflam. And I can not conceive of Peters Brown rejoicing at having thirty thousand of those dollars put into an In Memoriam to the women who sniffed at him and his carpetbags for a good twenty years after the war. But the child doesn't take any of that in. Those were twenty rich years he put in in reconstructing us, but when he took those same heavy carpetbags North he took Mary Caroline Darrah, the prettiest woman in the county with him. This girl—as I have said before, isn't love a strange thing? And you say the populace was astonished?"

"Almost to the point of paralyzation," answered David as he filled a stray pipe with some of the major's most choice heart-leaf tobacco. "But we managed to open up the picture show all right. The entire hive of busy art-bees was there in a queer kind of clothes; but proud of it. They acted as if we were dirt under their feet. They smiled on the whole glad-crowd of us with pity and let us rave over the wrong pictures. The portrait of Mrs. Peyton Kendrick by the great Susie Carrie Snow is—er—well, a little more of it shows than seems natural about the left off arm, but it's a Susie Carrie all right. You ought to have gone, Major, you would take with the art-gang, but we didn't; we were too afraid of them. After we had been shooed in front of most of the pictures and told how to see things in them that weren't there at all, Hob Capers said:

"'Let's all go down to the University Club and get drunk to forget 'em.' That's why Mrs. Matilda came home so late."

"And I want Hobson to be nice to her too," continued Mrs. Buchanan as if she had not been interrupted in planning for her guest. "And Tom and Peyton Kendrick. I'll ask them to come and see her right away."

"Don't! Wait a bit, Mrs. Matilda," exclaimed David. "Hob saw a mysterious girl in an orchid hat out in the park day before yesterday. He says his heart creaked with expansion at just the glimpse of a chin he got from under her veil. Suppose she's the girl. Let him have first innings."

"David," remarked the major, "flag the sun, moon and stars in their courses and signal time to reverse a day or a year, but don't try to turn aside a maker of matches from her machinations."

David laughed as the major's wife shook her head at him in gentle reproof, and he asked interestedly:

"When may we come to call, madam? I judge the lady is under your roof?"

"Soon, dear. She is very tired to-day, and I feel sure you will—"

"Miss Matilda," called Tempie from the hall, "Miss Phoebe is holdin' the phone fer you. She's at Mis' Cantrell's and she wants ter speak with you right away."

"Wait, wait, don't answer her right now—ring her off, Tempie! If she has trouble getting you, Mrs. Matilda, and you keep her talking I can catch her. Let me get a good start and then answer. Good-by! Keep talking to her!" And with determination in his eyes David took his hurried departure.

"Good-by, good luck—and good hunting!" called the major after him.

And with the greatest skilfulness Mrs. Buchanan held Phoebe in hand for enough minutes to insure David's capture before she returned to the library.

"Major," she said as she rubbed her cheek against his velvet coat sleeve, "why do you suppose Phoebe doesn't love David? I can't understand it."

"Matilda," answered the major as he blew a little curl over one of the soft puffs of her white hair, "you were born in a day when women were all run into a love-mold. They are poured into other assorted fancy shapes in these times, but heat from the right source melts them all the same. We can trust David's ardor, I think."

"Yes, I believe you are right," she answered judicially, "and Phoebe inherits lovingness from her mother. I feel that she is more affectionate than she shows, and I just go on and love her anyway. She lets me do it very often."

And from the depth of her unsophisticated heart Mrs. Buchanan had evolved a course of action that had gone far in comforting a number of the lonely years through which Phoebe Donelson had waded. She had been young, and high-spirited and intensely proud when she had begun to fight her own battles in her sixteenth year. Many loving hands of her mother's and father's old friends had been held out to her with a bounty of protection, but she had gone her course and carved her own fortune. Her social position had made things easy for her in a way and now her society editorship of the leading journal had become a position from which she wielded much power over the gay world that delighted in her wit and beauty, took her autocratic dictums in most cases, and followed her vogue almost absolutely.

Her independence prompted her to live alone in a smart down-town apartment with her old negro mammy, but her affections demanded that she take refuge at all times under the sheltering wings of Mrs. Buchanan, who kept a dainty nest always in readiness for her.

The tumultuous wooing of David Kildare had been going on since her early teens under the delighted eyes of the major, who in turn both furthered and hindered the suit by his extremely philosophical advice.

Phoebe was the crystallization of an infusion of the blood of many cultured, high-bred, haughty women which had been melted in the retort of a stern necessity and had come out a rather brilliant specimen of the modern woman, if a bit hard. Viewed in some ways she became an alarming augury of the future, but there are always potent counter-forces at work in life's laboratory, and the kind of forces that David Kildare brought to bear in his wooing were never exactly to be calculated upon. And so the major spent much time in the contemplation of the problem presented.

And when she had come in after a late lunch to call upon their guest, it had been intensely interesting to the major to regard the effect of the meeting of Phoebe's and Caroline Darrah's personalities. Caroline's lovely, shy child's eyes had melted with delight under Phoebe's straight, gray, friendly glances and her fascination for the tall, strong, radiant woman, who sat beside her, had been so obvious that the major had chuckled to himself under his breath as he watched them make friends, under Mrs. Matilda's poorly concealed anxiety that they should at once adopt cordial relations.

"And so he consented to undertake the commission for you because he was interested?" Phoebe was asking as they talked about the sketches of the statue. A very great sculptor was doing the work for Caroline Darrah Brown, and it interested Phoebe to hear how he had consented to accept so unimportant a commission.

"Yes," answered Caroline in her exquisite voice which showed only the faintest liquid trace of her southern inheritance. "I told him all about it and he became interested. He is very great, and simple, and kind. He made it easy to show him how I felt. I couldn't tell him much except how I felt; but I think it has something of—that—in—it. Don't you think so?" As she spoke she laid her white hand on the arm of Phoebe's chair and leaned forward with her dewy tender eyes looking straight into the gray ones opposite her.

For a moment Phoebe returned the glance with a quiet seriousness, then her eyes lighted a second, were suffused with a quick moisture, and with a proud gesture she bent forward, laying both hands on Caroline's shoulders as she pressed a deep kiss on the girl's red lips.

"I do think so," she answered with a low laugh as she arose to her feet, drew Caroline up into the bend of her arm and faced Mrs. Buchanan and the major. "I know the loveliness in the statue is what the great man got out of the loveliness in your heart, and the major and Mrs. Matilda think so, too. And I'm going quick because I must; and I'm coming back as soon as I can because I'm going to find you here—that is *partly*, Major," and before they could stop her she had gone on down the hall and they heard her answer Jeff's farewell as he let her out the door.

"That, Caroline Darrah Brown, was your first and most important conquest," observed the major. "Phoebe has a white rock heart but a crystal cracked therefrom is apt to turn into a jewel of price. Hers is a blood-ruby friendship that pays for the wearing and cherishing. But it's time for the nap Mrs. Matilda decides for me to take and I must leave you ladies to your dimity talk." With which he betook himself to his room, still plainly pleased at the result of Phoebe's call on the stranger.

The two women thus left to their own devices spent a delightful half-hour wandering over the house and discussing its furnishings and arrangements. Mrs. Buchanan never tired of the delights of her town home. The house was very stately and old-world, with its treasures of rare ancestral rosewood and mahogany that she had brought in from the Seven Oaks Plantation. The rooms in the country home had been so crowded with treasures of bygone generations that they were scarcely dismantled by the furnishing of the town house.

She was in her glory of domesticity, and as she passed from one room to another she told Caroline bits of interesting history about this piece or that. In her naiveté she let the girl see into the long hard years that had been a hand-to-hand struggle for her and the major on their worn farm lands out in the beautiful Harpeth Valley.

The cropping out of phosphate on the bare fields had brought a comfortable fortune in its train to the old soldier farmer and they had moved into this town house to spend the winter in greater accessibility to their friends. Her own particular little world had welcomed her with delight, and Caroline could see that she was taking a second bellehood as if it had been an uninterrupted reign.

Most of the financiers of the city were the major's old friends and they managed enormously advantageous contracts with mining companies for him, and had taken him into the schemes of the mighty with the most manifest cordiality.

His study became the scene of much important plot and counter-plot. They found in his mind the quality which had led them to outwit many an enemy when he scouted ahead of their tattered regiment, still available when the enemy appeared under commercial or civic front. Also it naturally happened that his library gradually became the hunting-grounds for Mrs. Matilda's young people, who were irresistibly drawn into the circle of his ever ready sympathy.

The whole tale and its telling was absorbingly interesting to Caroline Darrah Brown and she listened with enraptured attention to it all. She repeated carefully the names of her mother's friends as they came up in the conversation; and she was pathetically eager to know all about this world she had come back into, from, what already seemed to her, her birth in a strange land. Two days in this country of her mother, and the enchantment of traditions that had been given to her unborn was already at work with its spell!

And so they rambled around and talked, unheeding the time until the early twilight began to fall and Mrs. Buchanan was summoned by Jeff to a consultation in the domestic regions with the autocratic Tempie.

Left to herself, Caroline Darrah wandered back again through the rooms from one object to another that inspired the stories. It was like fairy-land to her and she was in a long dream of pleasure. Out of the shadows she seemed to be drawing her

Maria Thompson Daviess

wistful young mother, and hand in hand they were going over the past together.

When it was quite deep into the twilight she sauntered back to the crackling comfort of the major's fragrant logs. A discussion with Jeff over his toilet had delayed the major in his bedroom and she found the library deserted, but hospitable with firelight.

How long she had been musing and castle-building in the coals she scarcely knew, when a step on the polished floor made her look up, and with a little exclamation she rose to her full, slim, young height and turned to face a man who had come in with the unannounced surety of a member of the household. He was tall, broad and dark, and his knickerbockers were splashed with mud and covered with clinging burrs and pine-needles. One arm was lashed to his side with a silk sling and he held a huge bunch of glowing red berries in his free hand. They were branches of the red, coral-strung buck bushes and Caroline had never seen them before. Their gorgeousness fairly took her breath and she exclaimed with the ingenuous delight of a child.

"How lovely, how lovely!" she cried as she stretched out her hands for them. "I never saw any before. Do they grow here?"

"Yes," answered the man with a gleam of amusement in his dark eyes, "yes, they came from Seven Oaks. The fields are full of them now. Do you want them?" And as he spoke he laid the bunch in her arms.

"And they smell woodsy and piny and delicious. Thank you! I—they are lovely. I—" She paused in wild confusion, looked around the room as if in search of some one, and ended by burying her face in the berries. "I don't know where Major Buchanan is," she murmured helplessly.

"Well, it doesn't matter," he said with a comforting smile as he came up beside her on the rug. "They'll introduce us when they come. I'm Andrew Sevier and the berries are yours, so what matter?"

"Oh," said Caroline Darrah in an awed voice, and as she spoke she raised her head from the wood flowers and her eyes to his face, "oh, are you really Andrew Sevier?"

"Yes, *really*," he answered with another smile and a slightly puzzled expression in his own dark eyes.

"But I read everything I can find about you, and the papers say you are ill in Panama. I've been so worried about you. I saw your play last week in New York and I couldn't enjoy it for wondering how you were. I wouldn't read your poem in this month's *Review* because I was afraid you were dead—and I didn't know it. I'm so relieved." With which astonishing remark she drew a deep breath and laid her cheek against the field bouquet.

"I am—that is I was smashed up in Panama until David came down and brought me home. It was awfully good of you to—to know that I—that I—" Andrew Sevier paused as mirth, wonder and gratitude spread in confusion over his suntanned face.

"How did it happen? Was it very dreadful?" And again those distractingly solicitous eyes, full of sympathetic anxiety, were raised to his. Andrew shook himself mentally to see if it could possibly be a dream he was having, and a little thrill shot through him at the reality of it all.

"Nothing interesting; end of a bridge collapsed and put a rib or two out of commission," he managed to answer.

"I *knew* it was something dreadful," said Caroline Darrah Brown as she moved a step nearer him. "I was really unhappy about it and I wondered if all the other people who read your poems and watch for them and—and love them like I do, were worried, too. But I concluded that they would know how to find out about you; only I didn't. I'm glad you are here safe and that I know it."

The puzzled expression in Andrew Sevier's face deepened. Of course he had become more or less accustomed to the interest which his work had caused to be attached to his personality, and this was not the first time he had had a stranger read the poet into the man on first sight. They had even gone so far as to expect him to talk in blank verse he felt sure, especially when his admirer had been a member of the opposite and fair sex, but a thing like this had never happened to him before. It was, at the least, disturbing to have a lovely woman rise out of the major's very hearthstone and claim him as a familiar spirit with the exquisite frankness of a child. It smacked of the wine of wizardry. He glanced at her a moment and was on the point of making a tentative inquiry when the major came into the room.

"Well, Andy boy, you're in from the fields, I see. How's the farm? Every thing shipshape?" As he spoke the major shot a keen glance from under his beetling old brows at the pair and wisely let the situation develop itself.

Andrew answered his salutation promptly, then turned an amused glance on the girl at his side.

"He isn't going to introduce us," she laughed with a friendly little look up into his face. "I ought to have done it myself when you did, but I was so astonished—and relieved to find you. I'm Caroline Darrah Brown."

The words were low and laughing and warm with a sweet friendliness, but they crashed through the room like the breath of a swarm of furies. Andrew Sevier's face went white and drawn on the instant, and every muscle in his body stiffened to a tense rigidity. His dark eyes narrowed themselves to slits and glowed like the coals.

The major's very blood stopped in his veins and his fine old face looked drawn and gray as he stretched out his hand and laid it on Caroline's young shoulder. Not a word came to his lips as he looked in Andrew's face and waited.

And as he waited a wondrous thing and piercing sweet unfolded itself under his keen old eyes and sank like a balm into his wise old heart. From the two deep purple pools of womanhood that were raised to his, shy with homage of him and unconscious of their own tender reverencing, Andrew Sevier drew a deep draught into his very soul. Slowly the color mounted into his face, his eyes opened themselves and a wonderful smile curled his lips. He held out his hand and took her slender fingers into a strong clasp and held them for a long moment. Then with a smile at the major, which was a mixture of dignity tinged with an infinite sadness, he bent over and gently kissed the white hand as he let it go. The little ceremony had more chivalry than she understood.

"Its part of our ritual of welcome I'm claiming," he said lightly as she blushed rose pink and the divine shyness deepened in her eyes. She again buried her face in the berries.

Then with a proud look into Andrew's face the major laid his hand on the young man's bandaged arm and bent and raised Caroline's hand to his lips.

"It's a ritual, my dear," he said, "that I'm honored in observing with him. Friendship these days has need of rituals of ratification and the pomp of ceremonials to give it color. There's danger of its becoming prosaic. Jefferson, turn on the lights."

CHAPTER III

TWO LITTLE CRIMES

And then in a few weeks winter had come down from over the hills across the fields and captured the city streets with a blare of northern winds, which had been met and tempered by the mellow autumn breezes that had been slow to retreat and abandon the gold and crimson banners still fluttering on the trees. The snap and crackle of the Thanksgiving frost had melted into a long lazy silence of a few more Indian summer days so that, with lungs filled with the intoxicating draught of this late wine of October, everybody had ridden, driven, hunted, golfed and lived afield.

Then had come a second sweep of the northern winds and the city had wakened out of its haze of desertion, turned up its lights, built up its fires and put on the trappings of revelry and toil.

The major's logs were piled the higher and crackled the louder, and his welcome was even more genial to the chosen spirits which gathered around his library table. He and Mrs. Buchanan had succeeded in prolonging the visit of Caroline Darrah Brown into weeks and were now holding her into the winter months with loving insistence.

The open-armed hospitality with which their very delightful little world had welcomed her had been positively entrancing to the girl and she had entered into its gaieties with the joyous zest of the child that she was. Her own social experiences had been up to this time very limited, for she had come straight from the convent in France into the household of her semi-invalided father. He had had very few friends and in a vaguely uncomfortable way she had been made to realize that her millions made her position inaccessible; but by these delightful people to whom social position was a birthright, and wealth regarded only as a purchasing power for the necessities and gaieties of life, she had been adopted with much enthusiasm. Her delight in the round of entertainments in her honor and the innocent and slightly bewildered adventures she brought the major for consultation kept him in a constant state of interested amusement. Such advice as he offered went far in preserving her unsophistication.

And so the late November days found him enjoying life with a decidedly added zest in things, though his Immortals claimed him the moment he was left to his own resources and at times he even became entirely oblivious to the eddies in the lives around him. One cold afternoon he sat in his chair, buried eyes-deep in one of his old books, while across from him sat Phoebe and Andrew Sevier, bending together over a large map spread out before them. There were stacks of blueprints at their elbows and their conference had evidently been an interesting one.

"It's all wonderful, Andrew," Phoebe was saying, "and I'm proud indeed that they have accepted your solution of such an important construction problem; but why must you go back? Aren't the commissions offered you here, the plays and the demand for your writing enough? Why not stay at home for a year or two at least?"

"It's the *call* of it, Phoebe," he answered. "I get restless and there's nothing for it but the hard work of the camp. It's lonely but it has its compensations, for the visions come down there as they don't here. You know how I like to be with all of you; and it's home—but the depression gets more than I can stand at times and I must go. You understand better than the rest, I think, and I always count on you to help me off." As he spoke he rested his head on his hands and looked across the table into the fire. His eyes were somber and the strong lines in his face cut deep with a grim melancholy.

Phoebe's frank eyes softened as they looked at him. They had grown up together, friends in something of a like fortune and she understood him with a frank comradeship that comforted them both and went far to the distraction of young David Kildare who, as he said, trusted Andrew but looked for every possible surprising maneuver in the conduct of Phoebe. And because she understood Andrew Phoebe was silent for a time, tracing the lines on his map with a pencil.

"Then you'll have to go," she said softly at last, "but don't stay so long again." She glanced across at the top of the major's head which showed a rampant white lock over the edge of his book. "We miss you; and you owe it to some of us to come back oftener from now on."

"I always will," answered Andrew, quickly catching her meaning and smiling with a responsive tenderness in a glance at the absorbed old gentleman around the corner of the table. "It is harder to go this time than ever, in a way; and yet the staying's worse. I'm giving myself until spring, though I don't know why. I—"

Just then from the drawing-room beyond there came a crash of soft chords on the piano and David's voice rose high and sweet across the rooms. He had gone to the piano to sing for Caroline who never tired of his negro melodies and southern love songs. He also had a store of war ballads with which it delighted him to tease and regale her, but to-day his mood had been decidedly on the sentimental vein.

"I want no stars in Heaven to guide me,
I need no............................
but, oh, the kingdom of my heart, love,
Lies within thy loving arms...."

His voice dropped a note lower and the rest of the distinctly enunciated words failed to reach through the long rooms. Phoebe also failed to catch a quick breath that Andrew drew as he began stacking a pile of blue-prints into a leather case.

"David Kildare," remarked the old major as he looked up over his book, "makes song the vehicle of expression of as many emotions in one half-hour as the ordinary man lives through in a lifetime. Had you not better attend to the safeguarding of Caroline Darrah's unsophistication, Phoebe?"

"I wouldn't interrupt him for worlds, Major," laughed Phoebe as she arose from her chair. "I'm going to slip by the drawing-room and hurry down to that meeting of the Civic Improvement Association from which I hope to get at least a half column. Andrew'll go in and see to them."

"Never!" answered Andrew promptly with a smile. "I'm going to beat a retreat and walk down with you. The major must assume that responsibility. Good-by!" And in a moment they had both made their escape, to the major's vast amusement.

For the time being the music in the drawing-room had stopped and David and Caroline were deep in an animated conversation.

"The trouble about it is that I am about to have my light put out," David was complaining as he sat on the piano-stool, glaring at a vase of unoffending roses on a table. "Being a ray of sunshine around the house for a sick poet is no job for a runabout child like me."

"But he's so much better now, David, that I should think you would be perfectly happy. Though of course you are still a little uneasy about him." As Caroline Darrah spoke she swayed the long-stemmed rose she held in her hand and tipped it against one of its mates in the vase.

"Uneasy, nothing! There's not a thing in the world the matter with him; ribs are all in commission and his collar-bone hitched on again. It's just a case of moonie sulks with him. He never was the real glad boy, but now he runs entirely to poetry and gloom. He won't go anywhere but over here to chew book-rags with the major or to read goo to Phoebe, which she passes on to you. Wish I'd let him die in the swamps; chasing away to Panama for him was my mistake, I see." And David ruffled a young rose that drooped confidingly over toward him.

"Why did he ever go to Panama? Why does he build bridges and things? Other people like you and me can do that sort of thing; but he—," and Caroline Darrah raised her eyes full of naive questioning.

"Heavens, woman, poetry never in the world would grub-stake six feet of husky man! But that's just like you and Phoebe and all the other women. You would like to feed me to the alligators, but the poet must sit in the shade and chew eggs and grape juice. You trample on my feelings, child," and David sighed plaintively.

Caroline eyed him a moment across the rose she held to her lips, then laughed delightedly.

"Indeed, indeed, I couldn't stand losing you, David, nor could Phoebe. Don't imagine it!" And Caroline confessed her affection for him with the naïveté with which a child offers a flower.

The absolute entente cordiale which had existed between her and Phoebe from the moment Mrs. Buchanan had presented them to each other in the dusk-shadowed library, had been extended to include David Kildare. He was duly appreciative of her almost appealing friendship, chaffed her about the three governors, depended upon her to further his tumultuous suit, admired her beauty, insisted upon it in season and out, and initiated her into the social intricacies of his gay set with the greatest glee.

"I don't trust you one little bit, Caroline Darrah Brown," David broke in on her moment's silent appreciation of him and his friendliness. "You look at him kinder partial-like, too."

"Oh, one *must* admire him, his poems are so lovely! I have watched for them from the first one years ago. Do you remember the one where he—"

"Don't remember a single line of a single one, and don't want to! Phoebe's always quoting them at me. She's got a book of 'em. See if I don't smash him up some day if I have to listen to much more of it." David's face was a study in the contradictions of a tormented grin.

Caroline eyed him again for a moment across the rose and then they both laughed delightedly. But David was for the pressing of his point just the same.

"Dear Daughter of the Three," he pleaded, "can't you help me out? Mollycoddle him a bit. Do, now, that's a good child! Keep him 'interested', as *she* calls it! You are quite as good to look at as Phoebe and are enough more—more,"—and David paused for a word that would compare Caroline's appeal and Phoebe's brisk challenge.

"Yes, I understand. I really am *more* so; but how can I help you out if he never even sees me when I'm there?" And Caroline raised eyes to him that held a hint of wistfulness in their banter.

"The old mole-eyed grump never sees anybody nor anything. But let's plot a scheme. This three-handed game doesn't suit me; promise to be good and sit in. I haven't had Phoebe to myself for the long time. He needs a heart interest of his own—I'm tired of lending him mine. You're not busy—that's a sweet girl! Don't make me feel I inherited you for nothing," said David in a most beguiling voice as he moved a shade nearer to her.

"I promise, I promise! If you take that tone with me, I'm afraid not to: but I feel you mistake my powers," and Caroline laid the rose across her knee and dropped her long lashes over her eyes. "I think I'll fail with your poet; something tells me it is a vain task. Let's put it in the hands of the gods. It may interest them."

"No, I'm going to shoo him in here right now," answered David, bent upon the immediate accomplishment of his scheme for the relief of his very independent lady-love from her friendly durance. "You just wait and get a line of moon-talk ready for him. Keep that rose in your hand and handle your eyes carefully."

"Oh, but it's impossible!" exclaimed Caroline with real alarm in her voice. She rose and the flower fell shattered at her feet. "I'm going to have a little business talk with the major before Captain Cantrell and the other gentlemen come. I have an appointment with him. Won't you leave it to the gods?"

"No, for the gods might not know Phoebe. She'd hunt a hot brick for a sick kitten if I was freezing to death, and besides I need her in my business at this very moment."

"Caroline, my dear," said the major from the door into the library, "from the strenuosity in the tones of David Kildare I judge he is discussing his usual topic. Phoebe and Andrew have just gone and left their good-bys for you both."

"Now, Major," demanded David indignantly, "how could you let her get away when you had her here?"

"Young man," answered the major, "the constraining of a woman of these times is well-nigh impossible, as you should have found out after your repeated efforts in that direction."

"That's it, Major, you can't hang out any signal for them now; you have to grab them as they go past, swing out into space and pray for strength to hold on. I believe if you stood still they would come and feed out of your hand a heap quicker than they will be whistled down—if you can get the nerve to try 'em. Think I'll go and see." And David took his studiedly unhurried departure.

"David Kildare translates courtship into strange modern terms," remarked the major as he led Caroline into the library and seated her in Mrs. Matilda's low chair near his own.

"The roses are blooming this morning, my dear," he said, looking with delight at the soft color in her cheeks and the stars in her black-lashed, violet eyes. A shaft of sunlight glinted in the gold of her hair which was coiled low and from which little tendrils curled down on her white neck.

She was very dainty and lovely, was Caroline Darrah Brown, with the loveliness of a windflower and young with the innocent youngness of an April day. She was slightly different from any girl the major had ever known and he observed her type with the greatest interest.

She had been tutored and trained and French-convented and specialized by adepts in the inculcating of every air and grace with which the women of vaster wealth are expected to be equipped. Money and the girl had been the ruling passions of Peters Brown's life and the one had been all for the serving purposes of the other. It had been the one aim of his existence to bring to a perfect flowering the new-born bud his southern wife had left him, and he had succeeded. Yet she seemed so slight a woman-thing to be bearing the burden of a great wealth and a great loneliness that the major's eyes grew very tender as he asked:

"What is it, clear, a crumpled rose-leaf?"

"Major," she answered as her slender fingers opened and closed a book on the table near her, "did you realize that two months have passed since I came to—to—"

"Came *home*, child," prompted the major as he touched lightly the restless hand near his own.

"I am beginning to feel as if it might be that, and yet I don't know—not until I talk to you about it all. Everybody has been good to me. I feel that they really care and I love it—and them all! But, Major, did you—know—my father—well?"

"Yes, my dear." He answered, looking her straight in the eyes, "I knew Peters Brown and had pleasantly hostile relations with him always."

"This memorandum—I got it together before I came down here, while I was settling up his estate. It is the list of the investments he made while in the South for the twenty years after the war. I want to talk them over with you." She looked at the major squarely and determinedly.

"Fire away," he answered with courage in his voice that belied the feeling beneath it.

"I see that in eighteen seventy-nine he bought lumber lands from Hayes Donelson. The price seems to have been practically nominal in view of what he sold a part of them for three years later. Was Hayes Donelson Phoebe's father? I want to know all about him."

"My dear, you are giving a large order for ancient history—Captain Donelson couldn't fill it himself if he were alive. Those lumber lands were just a stick or two that he threw on the grand bonfire. He sold everything he had and instituted and ran the most inflammatory newspaper in the South. He gloried in an attitude of non-reconstruction and died when Phoebe was a year old. Her mother raised Phoebe by keeping boarders, but failed to raise the mortgage on the family home. She died trying and Phoebe has kept her own sleek little head above water since her sixteenth year by reporting and editing Dimity Doings on the paper her father founded. I think she has learned a pretty good swimming stroke by this time. It is still a measure ahead of that of David Kildare and—"

"Oh, you *must* help me make her take what would have been a fair price for those lands, Major. I'm determined—I—I—" Caroline's voice faltered but her head was well up. "I'm determined; but we'll talk of that later. He bought the Cantrell land and divided it up into the first improved city addition. Was it, was it 'carpetbagging'?" She flushed as she said the word—"Was it pressure? Were the Cantrells in need?"

"Not for long, my dear, not for long! Mrs. Tom took that money and bought cows for the east farm, ran a dairy in opposition to Matilda's and then got her into a combine to ship gilt-edge to Cincinnati. I expected them to skim the milky way any night and put a star brand of butter on the market. They made a great deal of money and were proportionately hard to manage. Young Tom inherits from his mother and makes paying combines in stocks. Old Tom hasn't a thing to do but sit in the sun and spin tales about battles he was and was not in. It wouldn't do to drag up that pinched period of his life; he is too expansive now to be made to recall it." The major smiled invitingly as if he had hopes of an interested question that would turn the trend of the conversation, but Caroline Darrah held herself sternly to the matter in hand.

"And you, I see a sale of half of your land at—"

"Caroline Darrah Brown, look me straight in the eyes," interrupted the major in a commanding voice. He sat up and bent his keen black eyes that sparkled under his heavy white brows with absolute luminosity upon the girl at his side. When aroused the major was a live wire and he was buckling on his sword to do battle with a woman-trouble, and a dire one.

"Now," he continued, "I'm going to say things to you that you are to understand and remember, young woman. Your father did come down among us with what you have heard called a 'carpetbag' in his hands, but it wasn't an *empty* one: and while the sums he handed out to each of us might be considered inadequate, still they were a purchasing power at a time when things were congested for the lack of any circulating medium whatever. True, I sold him half my thousand acres for a song; but the song fenced the other half, bought implements and stock, and made Matilda possible. She was eighteen and I was twenty-eight when we joined forces and it was decidedly to the tune of your father's 'song'. It was the same with the rest of his—friends. You must see that in the painful processes of reconstructing us the carpetbag had its uses. If it went away plethoric with coal and iron and lumber, it left a little gold in its wake. And Peters Brown—"

"Major," said Caroline in a brave voice, "it killed him, the memory of it and not being able to bring me back to her people. He was changed and he realized that he left me very much alone in the world. If there had been any of her immediate family alive we might have felt differently—but her friends—I didn't know that I would be welcomed. Now—now—I begin to hope. I want to give some of it back! I have so much—"

"Caroline, child," answered the major with a smile that was infinitely tender, "we don't need it! We've had a hand-to-hand fight to inherit the land of our fathers but we're building fortunes fast; we and the youngsters. The gray line has closed up its ranks and toed hard marks until it presents a solid front once more; some of it bent and shaky but supported on all sides by keen young blood. A solid front, I say, and a friendly one, flying no banners of bitterness—don't you like us?" and the smile broadened until it warmed the very blood in Caroline Darrah's heart.

"Yes," she said as she lifted her eyes to his and laid both her hands in the lean strong one he held out for her then, "and all that awful feeling has gone completely. I feel—feel new born!"

"And isn't it a great thing that we mortals are given a few extra natal days? If we were born all at one time we couldn't so well enjoy the processes. Now, I intend to assume that fate has laid you on my door-step and—"

"Dearie me," said Mrs. Buchanan as she sailed into the room with colors flying in cheeks and eyes, "did Phoebe go on to that meeting after all? Did she promise to come back? Where's Andrew? Caroline, child, what have you and the major been doing all the afternoon? It's after four and you are both still indoors."

"I have been adopting Caroline Darrah and she has been adopting me," answered the major as he caught hold of the lace that trailed from one of his wife's wrists. "I think I am about to persuade her to stay with us. I find I need attention occasionally and you are otherwise engaged for the winter."

"Isn't he awful, Caroline," smiled Mrs. Matilda as she sank for a moment on a chair near them, "when I haven't a thought in the day that is not for him? But I must hurry and tell Tempie that they will all be here from the philharmonic musicale for tea. Dear, please see that the flowers are arranged; I had to leave it to Jane this morning. I find I must run over and speak to Mrs. Shelby about something important, for a moment. Shall I have buttered biscuits or cake for tea? Caroline, love, just decide and tell Tempie. I'll be back in a minute," and depositing an airy kiss on the major's scalp lock and bestowing a smile on Caroline, she departed.

The major listened until he heard the front door close then said with one of his slow little smiles, "If I couldn't shut my eye and get a mental picture of her in a white sunbonnet with her skirts tucked up trudging along behind me dropping corn in the furrows as I opened them with the plow, I might feel that I ought to—er—remonstrate with her. But there are bubbles in the nature of most women that will rise to the surface as soon as the cork is removed. Matilda is a good brand of extra dry and the cork was in a long time—rammed down tight—bless her!"

"She is the very dearest thing I ever knew," answered Caroline with a curly smile around her tender mouth. "A letter she wrote while under the pressure of the cork is my chiefest treasure. It was written to welcome me when I was born and I found it last summer, old and yellow. It was what made me think I might come—*home*."

"That was like Matilda," answered the major with a smile in his eyes. "She was putting in a claim for you then, though she didn't realize it. Women have always worked combinations by wireless at long time and long distance. Better make it buttered biscuits, and Phoebe likes them with plenty of butter."

Tempie's adoption of Caroline Darrah had been as complete and as enthusiastic as the rest of them and she had proceeded forthwith to put her through a course of domestic instruction that delighted the hearts of them both. She never failed to bemoan the fate that had left the child ignorant of matters of such importance and she was stern in her endeavor to correct the pernicious neglect. She had to admit, however, that Caroline was an extraordinarily apt pupil and she laid it all to what she called "the Darrah strain of cooking blood," though she was as proud as possible over each triumph. Nothing pleased them both more than to have Mrs. Buchanan occasionally leave culinary arrangements to their co-administration.

An hour later a gay party was gathered around the table in the drawing-room. The major sat near at hand enjoying it hugely, and his comments were dropped like philosophical crystals into the swell of the conversation.

Mrs. Cherry Lawrence had come in with Mrs. Matilda in all the bravery of a most striking, becoming and expensive second mourning costume, and she was keenly alive to every situation that might be made to compass even the smallest amount of gaiety. Her lavender embroideries were the only reminders of the existence of the departed Cherry, and their lavishness was a direct defiance of his years of effort in the curtailing of the tastes of his expensive wife.

Tom Cantrell's lean dark face of Indian cast lit up like a transparency when she arrived and he left Polly Farrell's side so quickly that Polly almost dropped the lemon fork with which she was maneuvering, in her surprise at his sudden desertion. In a moment he had divested the widow of a long cloth and sable coat that would have made Cherry sit up and groan if he had even had a grave-dream about it. She bestowed a smile on Polly, a still more impressive one on the major and sank into a chair near Phoebe.

"Why, where is David Kildare?" she asked interestedly. "I thought he would be here before me. He promised to come. Phoebe, you are sweet in that dark gray. Has anybody anything interesting to tell?"

"I have," answered Polly as she passed Phoebe a cup and a mischievous smile, for Mrs. Cherry's appointment with David tickled Polly's risibles to an alarming extent. "There's the most heavenly man down here from Boston to see Caroline Darrah Brown and she *neglects* him. I'm so sorry for him that I don't know what will happen. I'm—"

"Why, where is he?" interrupted Mrs. Cherry with the utmost cordiality.

They all laughed as Polly parted her charming lips and passed the questioner the lemon slices with impressive obviousness.

"He's gone to the station to see about his horses that he has had shipped down. We're going to hunt some more, no matter how cold; all of us, Caroline and David and the rest."

"Andrew Sevier hasn't hunted at all this fall, as fond of it as he is. He'll never come now that you've annexed a foreign element, Polly. He's among strangers so much that he's rather absurd about wanting the close circle of just his old friends to be unbroken when he's home. Where is he to-day?" As she spoke Mrs. Cherry had looked at Caroline Darrah with a glance in which Phoebe detected a slight insolence and at which the major narrowed his observant eyes.

"Why, he's gone down to the station with Caroline's friend to see about having the horses sent out to Seven Oaks," answered Phoebe in a smooth cool voice. "I think all of us have been disappointed that Andrew has had to be so careful since his accident; but now that he can come over here every day to book gloat with the major and have Mrs. Matilda and Tempie, to say nothing of Caroline Darrah, the new star cook-lady, to feed him up, I think we can go about our own affairs unworried over him." The sweet smile that Phoebe bent upon the widow was so delicious that the major rattled the sugar tongs on the tea-tray by way of relief from an unendurably suppressed chuckle.

"But when I hunt next David has promised me possums and persimmons," said Caroline Darrah from her seat on the sofa beside Phoebe. She was totally oblivious of the small tongue-tilt just completed. "He says the first damp night on the last quarter of the moon when the wind is from the southeast and—"

"Howdy, people!" came an interrupting call from the hall and at that moment David himself came into the room. "I'm late but I've been four places hunting for you, Phoebe, and had three cups of tea in the scramble. However, I would like a buttered biscuit if somebody feeds it to me. I've had a knock-out blow and I've got news to tell."

"You can tell it before you get the biscuit," said Phoebe cold-heartedly, but she laid two crisp disks on the edge of his saucer. She apparently failed to see that Mrs. Cherry was endeavoring to pass him the plate.

"It's only that Milly Overton has perpetrated two more crimes on the community, at three-thirty to-day—assorted boy and girl." And David grinned with sheer delight at having projected such a bomb in the circle.

"What!" demanded Phoebe while Mrs. Cherry lay back in her chair and fanned herself, and Mrs. Buchanan paused with suspended teapot.

"Yes," he answered jubilantly, "Of course little Mistake is only two and a quarter and Crimie can just toddle on his hocks at one and a fifth years; but the two little crimes are here, and are going to stay. Billy Bob is down at the club getting his back slapped off about it. He's accessory you understand. He says Milly is radiant and wants all of you to come and see them right away. But what I want to see is Grandma Shelby—won't she rage? I'm going to send her a message of congratulations and then stand away. Just watch for—"

"Why—I don't quite understand," said Caroline Darrah as she leaned forward with puzzled eyes.

"Neither do any of the rest of us," answered David gleefully. "We didn't understand how Billy Bob managed to pluck Mildred from the golden-dollar Shelby stem in the first place, at a salary of one twenty-five a month out at Hob's mills. But Billy Bob is the brave boy and he marched right up and told the old lady about the first kid as soon as he came. Then she glared at him and said in an awful tone, 'Mistake.' Billy Bob just oozed out of that door and Mistake the youngster has been ever since. I named the next Crimie before *she* got to it. But watch her rage, poor old dame! It's up to somebody to remonstrate with Milly about this unbecoming conduct it seems to me," and David glanced around the little circle for his laugh which he promptly received.

Only Phoebe sat with her head turned from him and Caroline Darrah exclaimed in distress:

"How could her mother not care for them?"

"Tempie," said Mrs. Buchanan, "pack up a basket of every kind of jelly. Get that little box I fixed day before yesterday; you know it; wasn't it fortunate that I embroidered two? And tell Jeff I want the carriage at six."

"And, Tempie, tell Jeff to get you two bottles of that seventy-two brandy; no, maybe the sixty-eight will be better; it's apple, and apples and colic bear a synthetic relation which in this case may be reversed. Those children must be started off in life properly." And the major's eyes shone with the most amused interest.

"What's that?" asked David in the general excitement that had arisen at a farther realization of his news. "Don't you want them to join the 'state wide' band, Major? Aren't you going to give them a chance to fly a white ribbon?"

"Well, I don't know," answered the major with a judicial eye, "temperance is a quality of mind and not solely of throat. Let's depend somewhat on eradication by future education and not give the colic a start."

"Don't you think it would be nice for you girls to drive down with me and take the babies some congratulations and flowers, Phoebe?" asked Mrs. Buchanan an hour later as they all lingered over the empty cups. "Will you come too, David?"

"Yes," answered Phoebe, "I think it would be lovely, but you and Caroline drive down and I will walk in with David, I think. Ready, David?" And Phoebe gathered up her muff and gloves and gave her hand to the major.

"David," she said after they had reached the street and were swinging along in the early twilight; and as she spoke she looked him full in the face with her gray level glance that counted whenever she chose to use it, "is it your idea—do you think it fair to ridicule Mildred about—the babies?"

"Why," answered the completely floored Kildare, "I just haven't any idea on the subject. Everybody was laughing about it—and isn't it—er—a little funny?"

"No," answered Phoebe emphatically, "it isn't *funny* and if you begin to laugh everybody else will. It may hurt Milly, she is so gentle and dear, and you are their best friend. I won't have it! I won't! I'm tired, anyway, of having fun made of all the sacred things in life. All of us swing around in a silly whirl and when a woman like Mildred begins to live her life in a—er—natural way, we—ridicule! She is brave and strong and works hard; and she has the *real* things of life and makes the sacrifices for them. While we—"

"Oh, heavenly hope, Phoebe!" gasped David Kildare, "don't rub it in! I see it now—a lot of magazine stuff jogging the women up about the kids and all—and here Milly is a hero and we—the jolly fun-pokers. I've got to help 'em some way! Wish Billy Bob would sell me this last bunch; guess he would—one, anyway?" And the contrite David gazed down at Phoebe in whose upturned eyes there dawned a wealth of mirth.

"David," she said, perhaps more softly than she had ever spoken to him in all the days of his pursuit, "I know—I felt sure that you felt all right about it. I couldn't bear to have you say or do—"

"Now, I'll 'fess a thing to you that I didn't think wild horses could drag out of me, Phoebe. I was down there an hour ago in the back hall of that flat and Billy Bob let me hold the pair of 'em and squeeze 'em. I guess we both—just shed a few, you know, because he was so excited. Men are such slobs at times—when women don't know about it." And David winked fiercely at the early electric light that glowed warm against the winter sky.

"And you are a very dear boy, David," said Phoebe softly as her hand slipped out of her muff and dropped into his and rested there for just one enchanting half-second. "Dearer than you know in some ways. No, don't think of coming up with me, you've paid your visit of welcome. Good night! Yes, I think so—in the afternoon about three o'clock and we can go on to

Mrs. Pepton's reception. Good night again!"

"Phoebe," he called after her, "the one with the yellow fuzz is the girl, buy her for me if you can flimflam Milly into it! Any old price, you know. Hurrah, America for the Anglo-Saxons! Hurrah for Milly and Dixie!"

CHAPTER IV

ACCORDING TO SOLOMON

"And it was by this very pattern, Caroline, I made the dozen I sent Mary Caroline for you. See the little slips fold over and hold up the petticoats," and Mrs. Buchanan held up a tiny garment for Caroline Darrah to admire. They sat by the sunny window in her living-room and both were sewing on dainty cambric and lace. Caroline Darrah's head bent over the piece of ruffling in her hand with flower-like grace and the long lines from her throat suggested decidedly a very lovely Preraphaelite angel. Her needle moved slowly and unaccustomedly but she had the air of doing the hemming bravely if fearfully.

"Isn't it darling?" she said as she raised her head for a half-second, then immediately dropped her eyes and went on printing her stitches carefully. "What else was in that box, I feel I need to know?" she asked.

"Let me see! The dozen little shirts, they were made out of some of my own trousseau things because of a scarcity of linen in those days, and two little embroidered caps and a blue cashmere sack and a set of crocheted socks and—and the major sent brandy, he always does. I have the letter she wrote me about it all. And to think she had to leave—" Mrs. Matilda's eyes misted as she paused to thread her needle.

"She didn't realize—that, and think of what she felt when she opened the box," said Caroline as she raised her eyes that

Maria Thompson Daviess

smiled through a threatened shower. "Oh, I mustn't let the tears fall on Little Sister's ruffle!" she added quickly as she took up her work.

"That reminds me of an accident to the shirts I made for Phoebe. They were being bleached in the sun when a calf took a fancy to them and chewed two of them entirely up before we discovered him. I was so provoked, for I had no more linen as fine as I wanted."

"Of course the calf ate up my shirts," came in Phoebe's laughing voice from the doorway where she had been standing unobserved for several minutes, watching Mrs. Buchanan and Caroline. "Something is always chewing at my affairs but Mrs. Matilda shoos them away for me sometimes still—even *calve* when it is positively necessary. How very industrious you do look! At times even I sigh for a needle, though I wouldn't know what to do with it. There seems to be something in a woman's soul that nothing but a needle satisfies; morbid craving, that!"

"Phoebe, I want to make something for you. I feel I must as soon as these petticoats for Little Sister are done. What shall it be?" and Caroline Darrah beamed upon Phoebe with the warmest of inter-woman glances. The affection for Phoebe which had possessed the heart of Caroline Darrah had deepened daily and to its demands, Phoebe, for her, had been most unusually responsive.

"At your present rate of stitching I will have a year or two to decide, beautiful," she answered as she settled down on the broad window-seat near them. "David Kildare and I have come to lunch, Mrs. Matilda, and the major has sent him over for Andrew. I hope he brings him, but I doubt it. I have told Tempie and she says she is glad to have us," she added as Mrs. Buchanan turned and looked in the direction of the kitchen regions. They all smiled, for the understanding that existed between Phoebe and Tempie was the subject of continual jest.

"Have you seen the babies to-day?" asked Caroline as she drew a long new thread through the needle. "Isn't it lovely the way people are making them presents? Mr. Capers says the men at the mills are going to give them each a thousand dollar mill bond."

"Well, I doubt seriously if they will live to use the bonds if some one does not stop David from trying experiments with them," answered Phoebe with a laugh. "After dinner last night he came in with two little sleeping hammock machines which he insisted in putting up on the wall for them. If the pulley catches you have to stand on a chair to extract them; and if it slips, down they come. Milly was so grateful and let him play with them for an hour; she's a sweet soul."

"Has he sent any more food?" asked Mrs. Matilda as they all laughed.

"Two more cases of a new kind he saw advertised in a magazine. Somebody must tell him that—Milly is equal to the situation. Billy Bob *won't*; and so the cases continue to arrive. The pantry is crowded with them and they have sent a lot to the Day Nursery," and Phoebe slipped from the window-seat down on to the rug at Caroline's feet in a perfect ecstasy of mirth.

"But he is just the dearest boy, Phoebe," said Caroline Darrah as she paused in her sewing to caress the sleek, black, braided head tipped back against her knee. There was the shadow of reproach in her voice as she smiled down into the gray eyes upturned to hers.

"Yes," answered Phoebe, instantly on the defensive, "he is just exactly that, Caroline Darrah Brown—and he doesn't seem to be able to get over it. I'm afraid it's chronic with him."

"He's young yet," Mrs. Buchanan remarked as she clipped a thread with her bright scissors.

"No," said Phoebe slowly, "he is six years older than I am and that makes him thirty-two. I have earned my living for ten years and a man five years younger who sits at a desk next to mine at the office is taking care of his mother and educating two younger brothers on a salary that is less than mine—but *David* is a dear! Did you see the little coats Polly sent the babies?" she asked quickly to close the subject and to cover a note of pain she had discovered in her own voice.

"They were lovely," answered Mrs. Buchanan. "Now let me show you how to roll and whip your ruffle, Caroline dear," she added as she bent over Caroline's completed hem. In a moment they were both immersed in a scientific discussion of under-and-over stitch.

Phoebe clasped her knees in her arms and gazed into the fire. Her own involuntary summing up of David Kildare had struck into her inner consciousness like a blow. And Phoebe could not have explained to even herself what it was in her that demanded the hewer of wood and drawer of water in a man— in David. Decidedly Phoebe's demands were for elementals and she questioned Kildare's right to his leisurely life based on the Jeffersonian ideals of his forefathers.

And while they sewed and chatted the hour away, over in the library the major and David were in interested conclave.

"Now, I leave it to you, Major, if he isn't just the limit," said David on his return from his mission for the purpose of drawing Andrew from his lair. "I couldn't budge him. He is writing away like all possessed with a two-apple-and-a-cracker lunch on the table beside him. He seems to enjoy a death-starve."

"David," said the major as he laid aside the book he had been buried in and began to polish his glasses, "you make no allowances whatever for the artistic temperament. When a man is making connection with his solar plexus he doesn't consider the consumption of food of paramount importance. Now in this treatise of Aristotle—"

"Well, anyway, I've made up my mind to fix up something between him and Caroline Darrah. He's got to get a heart interest of his own and let mine alone. The child is daffy about his poetry and moons at him all the time out of the corners of her eyes, dandy eyes at that; but the old ink-swiller acts as if she wasn't there at all. What'll I do to make him just see her? Just see her—*see her*—that'll be enough!"

"David," said the major quietly as he looked into the fire with his shaggy brows bent over his keen eyes, "the combination of a man heart and a woman heart makes a dangerous explosive at the best, but here are things that make it fatal. The one you are planning would be deadly."

"Why, why in the world shouldn't I touch them off? Perfectly nice girl, all right man and—"

"Boy, have you forgotten that I told you of the night Andrew Sevier's father killed himself; yes, that he had sat the night through at the poker table with Peters Brown? Brown offered some restoration compromise to the widow but she refused—you know the struggle that she made and that it killed her. We both know the grit it took for Andrew to chisel himself into what he is. The first afternoon he met the girl in here, right by this table, for an instant I was frightened—only *she* didn't know, thank God! The Almighty gardens His women-things well and fends off influences that shrivel; it behooves men to do the same."

"So that's it," exclaimed Kildare, serious in his dismay. "Of course I remember it, but I had forgotten to connect up the circumstances. It's a mine all right, Major—and the poor little girl! She reads his poetry with Phoebe and to me and she admires him and is deferential and—that girl—the sweetest thing that ever happened! I don't know whether to go over and smash him or to cry on his collar."

"Dave," answered the major as he folded his hands and looked off across the housetops glowing in the winter sun, "some snarls in our life-lines only the Almighty can unravel; He just depends on us to keep hands off. Andrew is a fine product of disastrous circumstances. A man who can build a bridge, tunnel a mountain and then sit down by a construction camp-fire at night and write a poem and a play, must cut deep lines in life and he'll not cut them in a woman's heart—if he can help it."

"And she must never know, Major, *never*," said David with distress in his happy eyes; "we must see to that. It ought to be easy to keep. It was so long ago that nobody remembers it. But wait—that is what Mrs. Cherry Lawrence meant when she said to Phoebe in Caroline's presence that it was just as well under the circumstances that the committee had not asked Andrew to write the poem for the unveiling of the statue. I wondered at the time why Phoebe dealt her such a knock-out glance that even I staggered. And she's given her cold-storage attentions ever since. Mrs. Cherry rather fancies Andy, I gather. Would she dare, do you think?"

"Women," remarked the major dryly, "when man-stalking make very cruel enemies for the weaker of their kind. Let's be thankful that pursuit is a perverted instinct in them that happens seldom. We can trust much to Phoebe. The Almighty puts the instinct for mother guarding all younger or lesser women into the heart of superbly sexed women like Phoebe Donelson, and with her aroused we may be able to keep it from the child."

"Ah, but it is sad, Major," said David in a low voice deeply moved with emotion. "Sad for her who does not know—and for him who does."

"And it was farther reaching than that, Dave," answered the major slowly, and the hand that held the dying pipe trembled against the table. "Andrew Sevier was a loss to us all at the time and to you for whom we builded. The youngest and strongest and best of us had been mowed down before a four-years' rain of bullets and there were few enough of us left to build again. And of us all he had the most constructive power. With the same buoyant courage that he had led our regiment in battle did he lead the remnant of us in reconstructing our lives. He was gay and optimistic, laughed at bitterness and worked with infectious spirits and superb force. We all depended on him and followed him keenly. We loved him and let ourselves be laughed into his schemes. It was his high spirits and temperament that led to his gaming and tragedy. Nearly thirty years he's been dead, the happy Andrew. This boy's like him, very like him."

"I see it—I see it," answered David slowly, "and all of that glad heart was bred in Andy, Major, and it's there under his sadness. Heavens, haven't I seen it in the hunting field as he landed over six stiff bars on a fast horse? It's in some of his writing and sometimes it flashes in his eyes when he is excited. I've seen it there lately more often than ever before. God, Major, last night his eyes fairly danced when I plagued Caroline into asking him to whom he wrote that serenade which I have set to music and sing for her so often. It hurts me all over—it makes me weak—"

"It's hunger, David, lunch is almost ready," said Phoebe who had come into the room in time to catch his last words. "Why, where is Andrew? Wouldn't he come?"

"No," answered Kildare quickly, covering his emotion with a laugh as he refused to meet Caroline Darrah's eyes which wistfully asked the same question that Phoebe had voiced, "he is writing a poem—about—-about," his eyes roamed the room wildly for he had got into it, and his stock of original poem-subjects was very short. Finally his music lore yielded a point, "It's about a girl drinking—only with her eyes you understand—and—"

"He could save himself that trouble," laughed Phoebe, "for somebody has already written that; did it some time ago. Run stop him, David."

"No," answered David with recovered spirit, "I'd flag a train for you, Phoebe, but I don't intend to side-track a poem for anybody. Besides, I'm hungry and I see Jeff with a tray. Mrs. Matilda, please put Caroline Darrah by me. She's attentive and Phoebe just diets—me."

And while they laughed and chatted and feasted the hour away, across the street Andrew sat with his eyes looking over on to the major's red roof which was shrouded in a mist of yesterdays through which he was watching a slender boy toil his way. When he was eight he had carried a long route of the daily paper and he could feel now the chill dark air out into which he had slipped as his mother stood at the door and watched him down the street with sad and hungry eyes, the gaunt mother who had never smiled. He had fought and punched and scuffled in the dawn for his bundle of papers; and he had fought and scuffled for all he had got of life for many years. But a result had come—and it was rich. How he had managed an education he could hardly see himself; only the major had helped. Not much, but just enough to make it possible. And David had always stood by.

Kildare's fortune had come from some almost forgotten lumber lands that his father had failed to heave into the Confederate maelstrom. Perhaps it had come a little soon for the very best upbuilding of the character of David Kildare, but he had stood shoulder to shoulder with them all in the fight for the establishment of the new order of things and his generosity with himself and his wealth had been superb. The delight with which he made a gift of himself to any cause whatsoever, rather tended to blight the prospects of what might have been a brilliant career at law. With his backing Hobson Capers had opened the cotton mills on a margin of no capital and much grit. Then Tom Cantrell had begun stock manipulations on a few blocks of gas and water, which his mother and Andrew had put up the money to buy—and nerve.

It was good to think of them all now in the perspective of the then. Were there any people on earth who could swing the pendulum like those scions of the wilderness cavaliers and do it with such dignity? He was tasting an aftermath and he found it sweet—only the bitterness that had killed his mother before he was ten. And across the street sat the daughter of the man who had pressed the cup to her lips—with her father's millions and her mother's purple eyes.

He dropped his hand on his manuscript and began to write feverishly. Then in a moment he paused. The Panama campfire, beside which he had written his first play, that was running in New York now, rose in a vision. Was it any wonder that the managers had jumped at the chance to produce the first drama from the country's newly acquired jungle? The lines had been rife with the struggle and intrigue of the great canal cutting. It really was a ripping play he told himself with a smile—and this other? He looked at it a moment in a detached way. This other throbbed.

He gathered the papers together in his hand and walked to the window. The sun was now aslant through the trees. It was late and they must have all gone their ways from across the street; only the major would be alone and appreciative. Andrew smiled quizzically as he regarded the pages in his hand—but it was all so to the good to read the stuff to the old fellow with his Immortals ranged round!

"Great company that," he mused to himself as he let himself out of the apartment. And as he walked slowly across the street and into the Buchanan house, Fate took up the hand of Andrew Sevier and ranged his trumps for a new game.

In the moment he parted the curtains and stepped into the library the old dame played a small signal, for there, in the major's wide chair, sat Caroline Darrah Brown with her head bent over a large volume spread open upon the table.

"Oh," she said with a quick smile and a rose signal in her

Maria Thompson Daviess

cheeks, "the major isn't here! They came for him to go out to the farm to see about—about grinding something up to feed to—to—something or sheep—or—," she paused in distress as if it were of the utmost importance that she should inform him of the major's absence.

"Silo for the cows," he prompted in a practical voice. It was well a practical remark fitted the occasion for the line from old Ben Jonson, which David had only a few hours ago accused him of plagiarizing, rose to the surface of his mind. Such deep wells of eyes he had never looked into in all his life before, and they were as ever, filled to the brim with reverence, even awe of him. It was a heady draught he quaffed before she looked down and answered his laconic remark.

"Yes," she said, "that was it. And Mrs. Matilda and Phoebe motored out with him and David went on his horse. I am making calls, only I didn't. I stopped to—" and she glanced down with wild confusion, for the book spread out before her was the major's old family Bible, and the type was too bold to fail to declare its identity to his quick glance.

"Don't worry," he hastened to say, "I don't mind. I read it myself sometimes, when I'm in a certain mood."

"It was for David—he wanted to read something to Phoebe," she answered in ravishing confusion, and pointed to the open page.

Thus Andrew Sevier was forced by old Fate to come near her and bend with her over the book. The tip of her exquisite finger ran along the lines that have figured in the woman question for many an age.

"For her price is far above rubies. The heart of her husband doth safely trust in her"—and so on down the page she led him.

"And that was what the trouble was about," she said when they had read the last word in the last line. She raised her eyes to his with laughter in their depths. "It was a very dreadful battle and Phoebe won. The major found this for him to read to her and she said she did not intend to go into the real estate business for her husband or to rise while it was yet night to give him his breakfast. Aren't they funny, *funny*?" and she fairly rippled with delight at her recollection of the vanquishing of the intrepid David.

"The standards for a wife were a bit strenuous in those days," he answered, smiling down on her. "I'm afraid Dave will have trouble finding one on those terms. And yet—" he paused and there was a touch of mockery in his tone.

"I think that a woman could be very, very happy fulfilling every one of those conditions if she were woman enough," answered Caroline Darrah Brown, looking straight into his eyes with her beautiful, disconcerting, dangerous young seriousness.

Andrew picked up his manuscript with the mental attitude of catching at a straw.

"Oh," she said quickly, "you were going to read to the major, weren't you?" And the entreaty in her eyes was as young as her seriousness; as young as that of a very little girl begging for a wonder tale. The heart of a man may be of stone but even flint flies a spark.

Andrew Sevier flushed under his pallor and ruffled his pages back to a serenade he had written, with which the star for whom the play was being made expected to exploit a deep-timbred voice in a recitative vocalization. And while he read it to her slowly, Fate finessed on the third round.

And so the major found them an hour or more later, he standing in the failing light turning the pages and she looking up at him, listening, with her cheek upon her interlaced fingers and her elbows resting on the old book. The old gentleman stood at the door a long time before he interrupted them and after Andrew had gone down to put Caroline into her motorcar, which had been waiting for hours, he lingered at the window looking out into the dusk.

"For love is as strong as death," he quoted to himself as he turned to the table and slowly closed the book and returned it to its place. "And many waters can not quench love, neither can the floods drown it." "Solomon was very great—and human," he further observed.

Then after absorbing an hour or two of communion with some musty old papers and a tattered volume of uncertain age, the major was interrupted by Mrs. Matilda as she came in from her drive. She was a vision in her soft gray reception gown, and her gray hat, with its white velvet rose, was tipped over her face at an angle that denoted the spirit of adventure.

"I'm so glad to get back, Major," she said as she stood and regarded him with affection beaming in her bright eyes. "Sometimes I hurry home to be sure you are safe here. I don't see you as much as I do out at Seven Oaks and I'm lonely going places away from you."

"Don't you know it isn't the style any longer for a woman to carry her husband in her pocket, Matilda," he answered. "What would Mrs. Cherry Lawrence think of you?"

Mrs. Buchanan laughed as she seated herself by him for the moment. "I've just come from Milly's," she said. "I left Caroline there. And Hobson was with her; they had been out motoring on the River Road. Do you suppose—it looks as if perhaps—?"

"My dear Matilda," answered the major, "I never give or take a tip on a love race. The Almighty endows women with inscrutable eyes and the smile of the Sphynx for purposes of self-preservation, I take it, so a man wastes time trying to solve a woman-riddle. However, Hobson Capers is running a risk of losing much valuable time is the guess I chance on the issue in question."

"And Peyton Kendrick and that nice Yankee boy and—"

"All bunched, all bunched at the second post! There's a dark horse running and he doesn't know it himself. God help him!" he added under his breath as she turned to speak to Tempie.

"If you don't want her to marry Hobson whom do you choose?" she said returning to the subject. "I wish—I wish— but of course it is impossible, and I'm glad, as it is, that Andrew is indifferent."

"Yes," answered the major, "and you'll find that indifference is a hall mark stamped on most modern emotions."

CHAPTER V

DAVID'S ROSE AND SOME THORNS

"Now," said David, "if you'll just put away a few of those ancient pipes and puddle your papers a bit in your own cozy corner we can call these quarters ready to receive the ladies, God bless 'em! Does it look kinder bare to you? We might borrow a few drapes from the madam, or would you trust to the flowers? I'll send them up for you to fix around tasty. A blasted poet ought to know how to bunch spinach to look well."

As he spoke David Kildare stood in the middle of the living-room in his bachelor quarters, which were in the Colonial, a tall pillared, wide windowed, white brick apartment-house that stood across the street from the home of Major Buchanan, and surveyed the long rooms upon which he and his man Eph had been expending their energies for more than an hour.

Andrew Sevier sank down upon the arm of a chair and lighted a long and villainous pipe. "Trust to the flowers," he answered. "I think Phoebe doesn't care for the drapes of this life so much as some women do and as this is for her birthday let's have the flowers, sturdy ones with stiff stems and good head pieces."

"That's right, Phoebe's nobody's clinging vine," answered David moodily. "She doesn't want any trellis either—wish something would wilt her! Look here, Andrew, on the square, what's the matter that I can't get Phoebe? You're a regular love pilot on paper, point me another course; this one is no good; I've run into a sand bank." The dark red forelock on David's brow was ruffled and his keen eyes were troubled, while his large sweet mouth was set in a straight firm line. He looked very strong, forceful and determined as he stopped in front of his friend and squared himself as if for a blow.

Andrew Sevier looked at him thoughtfully for a few seconds straight between the eyes, then his mouth widened into an affectionate smile as he laid his hand on the sturdy shoulder and said:

"Not a thing on God's green earth the matter with you, Davie; it's the modernism of the situation that you seem unable to handle. May I use your flower simile? Once they grew in gardens and were drooping and sweet and overran trellises, to say nothing of clinging to oak trees, but we've developed the American Beauty, old man! It stands stiff and glossy and holds its head up on its own stem, the pride of the nation! We can get them, though they come high. Ah, but they are sweet! Phoebe is one of the most gorgeous to be found—it will be a price to pay, but you'll pay it, David, you'll pay."

"God knows I'm paying it all day long every day and have been paying it for ten years. Never at peace about her for an instant. Protection at long distance is no joke. I can't sleep at night until she telephones me she is at home from the office on her duty nights and then I have to beg like a dog for the wire, just the word or two. She *will* overwork and undereat and—"

"David," interrupted Sevier thoughtfully, "what do you really think is the matter? Let's get down to facts while we are about it."

"Do you know, Andy, lately it has dawned upon me that Phoebe would like to dictate a life policy to me; hand me out a good, stiff life job. I believe she would marry me to-morrow if she could see me permanently installed on the front seat of a grocery wagon—*permanently*. And I'll come to it yet."

"I believe you are right," laughed Andrew. "She really glories in her wage earning; it's a phase of them these days. She would actually hate living on your income."

"Don't I know it? I suppose she would be content if she sewed on buttons and did the family wash to conserve the delivery wagon income. I wish she'd marry me for love and then I'd hire her at hundreds per week to dust around the house and cook pies for me, gladly, gladly."

"We've developed thorns with our new rose, Dave," chuckled Andrew as he relighted his pipe.

"Sweet hope of heaven, yes," groaned David. "My gore drips all the time from the gashes. I suppose it is a killing grief to her that I haven't a star corporation practise instead of fooling around the criminal court fighting old Taylor to get a square deal for the darky rag-tag most of my time. But, Andy, it makes me blaze house-high to see the way he hands the law out to 'em. They can cut and fight as long as it is in a whisky dive and no indictment returned; but let one of 'em sidestep an inch in any other ignorant pitiful way and it's the workhouse and the county road for theirs.

"And the number of ways that the coons can get up to call on me to square the deal, is amazing. Just look at the week I've had! All Monday and Tuesday I spent on the Darky Country Club affair; the poor nigs just hungering for some place to go off and act white in for a few hours. Nobody would sell them an acre of ground near a car line and the dusky smart set was about to get its light put out. Jeff and Tempie told me about it. What did little Dave do but run around to persuade old man Elton to sell them that little point that juts out into the river two miles from town and just across from the rock quarry. No neighbors to kick and the interurban runs through the field. It really is a choice spot and I started their subscription with a hundred or two and got Williams to draw them some plans to fix up an old house that stands on the bank for a club-house. They are wide-mouthed with joy; but it sliced two days to do it, which I might have spent on the grocery wagon."

"You always did have the making of a philanthropist in you, Dave," said Andrew thoughtfully. "You're a near-one at present speaking."

"Philanthropist go hang—the rest of the week I have spent getting the old Confeds together and having everything in shape for the unveiling of the statue out at the Temple of Arts. I tell you we are going to have a turn-out. General Clopton is coming all the way to make the dedication speech. Caroline is about to bolt and I have to steady her at off times. I've promised to hold her hand through it all. Major is getting up the notes for General Clopton and he's touching on Peters Brown only in high places. It'll be mostly a show-down of old General Darrah and the three governors I'm thinking.

"The Dames of the Confederacy and the Art League are going to have entries on the program without number. I have been interviewed and interviewed. Why, even the august Susie Carrie Snow sent for me and talked high art and city beautiful to me until I could taste it.

"And all that sopped up the rest of the week when I ought to have been delivering pork steaks and string-beans at people's back doors to please Phoebe. Money grubbing doesn't appeal to me and I don't need it, but from now on I'm the busy grub—until after the 'no man put asunder' proclamation."

"How you can manage to do one really public-spirited job after another, 'things that count,' and then elude all the credit for them is more than I can understand, Dave," said Andrew as he smiled through a blue ring of smoke. "Some day, if you don't look out, you'll be a leading citizen. In the meantime hustle about those flowers. Time flies."

"I'll send them right up," said David as he donned his coat and hat and took up his crop. The hours David spent out of the saddle were those of his indoors occupations. "I'll be back soon. Just fix the flowers; Eph and the cook will do all the rest. And put the cards on the table any old way. I want to sit between Phoebe and Caroline Darrah Brown—well, whose party is it? You can sit next on either side."

"Wait a minute, are—"

"No, I must hurry and go brace up Milly for a pair of minutes. She wouldn't promise to come until I insisted on sending a trained nurse to sit with old Mammy Betty and the babies until she got back to 'em. Billy Bob is as wild as a kid about coming, he hasn't been anywhere for so long. I talked a week before I could persuade Milly, but she's got her glad rags and is as excited as Billy Bob. I tried to buy that boy twin for Phoebe's present but Milly said I had better get an old silver and amethyst bracelet. It's on my table in the white box. Bye!" and Kildare departed as far as the front door, but returned to stick his head in the door and say:

"You'd better put Hob by Caroline Darrah on the other side; he's savage when he's crossed. And tack in Payt opposite her. I invited Polly the Fluff for you—she is a débutante and such a coo-child that she'll just suit a poet."

He dodged just in time to escape the lighted pipe that was hurled upon him, and he couldn't have suspected that a hastily-formed plan to place himself opposite Caroline Darrah had gone up in the smoke that followed the death of life in Andrew's pipe.

Then following the urgent instructions of David, Andrew began to right up the papers in his den which opened off the living-room. His desk was littered with manuscript, for the three days past had been golden ones and he had written under a strong impetus. The thought suddenly shot through him that he had been writing as he had once read, to eyes whose "depths on depths of luster" had misted and glowed and answered as he turned his pages in the twilight. Can ice in a man's breast burn like fire? Andrew crushed the sheets and thrust them into a drawer.

Then came Eph and the cook to lay the cloth in the dining-room, and a man brought up the flowers. For a time he worked away with a strange excitement in his veins.

When they had finished and he was alone in the apartment he walked slowly through the rooms. Where David happened to keep his household gods had been home to Andrew for many years. His books were in the dark Flemish oak cases and some of the prints on the walls were his. Most of the rugs he had picked up in his travels upon which his commissions led him, and some interesting skins had been added since his jungle experiences. It was all dark and rich and right-toned—the home of a gentleman. And David was like the rooms, right-toned and clean.

Andrew found himself wondering if there would be men like David in the next generation, happy David with his cavalier nature and modern wit. The steady stream of wealth that was pouring into the South, down her mountain sides and welling up under her pasture lands, would it bring in its train death to the purity and sanity of her social institutions? Would swollen fortunes bring congestion of standards and grossness of morals? Suddenly he smiled for Billy Bob and Milly and a lot of the industrious young folks seemed to answer him. He had found eleven little new cousins on the scene of action when he had returned after five years—clear-eyed young Anglo-Americans, ready to take charge of the future.

And he, what was his place in the building of his native city? His trained intelligence, his wide experience, his genius were being given to cutting a canal thousands of miles away while the streets of his own home were being cut up and undermined by half-trained bunglers. The beautiful forest suburbs were being planned and plotted by money-mad schemers who neither pre-visioned, nor cared to, the city of the future which was to be a great gateway of the nation to its Panama world-artery. He knew how to value the force of a man of his kind, with his reputation and influence, and he would gage just what he would be able to do for the city with the municipal backing he could command if he set his shoulder to the wheel.

A talk he had had with the major a day or two ago came back to him. The old fellow's eyes had glowed as he told him the plan they had been obliged to abandon in the early seventies for a boulevard from the capitol to the river because of the lack of city construction funds. Andrew's own father had formulated the plan and gone before the city fathers with it, and for a time there had been hope of its accomplishment. And the major had declared emphatically that a time was coming when the city would want and ask for it again. That other Andrew Sevier of the major's youth had conceived the scheme; the major had repeated the fact slowly. Did he mean it as a call to him?

Andrew's eyes glowed. He could see it all, with its difficulties and its possibilities. He rested his clenched hand on the table and the artist in him had the run of his pulses. He could see it all and he knew in all humbleness that he could construct the town as no other man of his generation would be able to do; the beautiful hill-rimmed city!

And just as potent he felt the call of the half-awakened spirit of art and letters that had lain among them poverty-bound for forty reconstructive years. For what had he been so richly dowered? To sing his songs from the camp of a wanderer and write his plays with a foreign flavor, when he might voice his own people in the world of letters, his own with their background of traditions and tragedy and their foreground of rough-hewn possibilities? Was not the meed of his fame, small or large, theirs?

Suddenly the tension snapped and sadness chilled through his veins. Here there would always be that memory which brought its influences of bitterness and depression to kill the creative in him. The old mad desire to be gone and away from it beat up into his blood, then stilled on the instant. What was it that caught his breath in his breast at the thought of exile? Could he go now, *could*—

Just at this moment he was interrupted by Mrs. Matilda who came hurrying into the room with ribbons and veil aflutter. She evidently had only the moment to stay and she took in his decorative schemes with the utmost delight.

"Andrew," she said with enthusiasm in every tone, "it is all lovely, lovely. You boys are wonders! These bachelor establishments are threatening to make women wonder what they were born for. And what do you think? The major is coming! The first place he has gone this winter—and he wants to sit between Phoebe and Caroline Darrah. I just ran over to tell you. Good-by! We must both dress."

And Andrew smiled as he rearranged the place-cards.

And it happened that in more ways than one David Kildare found himself the perturbed host. He rushed home and dressed with lightning-like rapidity and whirled away in the limousine for Milly and Billy Bob. He went for them early, for he had bargained to come for Phoebe as late as possible so as to give her time to reckon with her six-thirty freckled-faced devil at the office. But at the Overtons he found confusion confounded.

"I'm so sorry, David," Milly almost sobbed, "but Mammy Betty's daughter has run away and got married and she has gone to see about it, and the trained nurse can't come. There has been an awful wreck up the road and all the doctors in town have gone and taken all the nurses with them. She didn't consider the babies serious, so she just had some one telephone at the last minute that she had gone. I can't go; but please make Billy go with you! There is no use—" and she turned to Billy Bob who stood by in pathetically gorgeous array, but firm in his intention not to desert the home craft.

Maria Thompson Daviess

"We just can't make it, Dave, old man," he said manfully, as he caught his tearful wife's outstretched hand in his. "Go on before we both cry!"

"Go on, nothing—with Milly looking like a lovely pink apple-blossom! You've got to come. I wouldn't dare face Phoebe without you. It's the whole thing to her to have you there. It's been so long since you've gladded with the crowd once and it's her birthday and—" David's voice trailed off into a perfect wail.

"But what can we do?" faltered Milly, dissolved at the mention of the new frock. "We certainly can't leave them and we can't take them and—"

"Glory, that's the idea, let's *take* the whole bunch!" exclaimed David with radiant countenance. "I ought to have invited them in the first place. Come on and let's begin to bundle!" and he made a dive in the direction of the door of the nursery.

"Oh, no, indeed we can't!" gasped Milly while Billy Bob stood stricken, unable to utter a word.

"I'll show you whether we will or not," answered David. "Catch me losing a chance like this to ring one on Phoebe for several reasons. Hurry up!" and as he spoke he had lifted little Mistake from his cot and was dextrously winding him in his blanket. The youngster opened his big dewy eyes and chuckled at the sight of his side partner, David Kildare.

"That's all right, he's all for his Uncle Davie. Here, you take him Billy Bob and I'll help Milly roll up the twins. She can bring down Crimie while I bring them," and as he spoke he began a rapid swathing of the two limp little bodies from the white crib.

"But, David," gasped Milly, "it is *impossible*! They are not dressed—they will take cold—"

"The limousine is as hot as smoke—can't hurt 'em—plenty of blankets," with which he thrust the nodding young Crimie into her arms and lifted carefully the large bundle which contained both twins in his own. "Go on!" he commanded the paralyzed pair. "I will pull the door to with my free foot." And he actually forced the helpless parents of the four to embark with him on this most unusual of adventures.

When they were all seated in the car Milly looked at Billy Bob and burst into a gale of hysterical laughter. But Billy Bob's spunk was up by this time and he was all on the side of the resourceful David.

"Why not?" he asked brazenly. "Nine-tenths of the people in the world take the kids with them on all the frolics they get, why not we? *They* know it's all right, *they* haven't objected." And indeed there had not been a single chirp from any of the swathings. Big Brother was the only one awake and he was, as usual, entranced at the very sight of his Uncle David, who held the twins with practised skill on his knees.

"Now," he said jubilantly, "don't anybody warn Phoebe and I'm going to put them on the big divan with her presents. You'll see something crash, I'm thinking."

And it was worth it all when Phoebe did see her unexpected guests. Big Brother, divested of his blanket and clad in a pink Teddy Bear garment, sat bolt upright in the center of the divan, and Crimie lay snuggled against him with his thumb in his mouth and entranced eyes on the brilliant chandelier. The twins were nestled contentedly down in the corner together like two little kittens in a basket. Before them knelt Polly with one finger clasped by the one whose golden fuzz declared her to be Little Sister, while Caroline Darrah leaned over Big Brother who was fingering a string of sapphires that fell from her neck, with obvious delight. The rest of the party stood in an admiring and uproarious circle.

"Why," exclaimed Phoebe in blank astonishment, "why

David Kildare!"

"You said you wanted your most intimate friends to-night, Phoebe, and here they are," he answered with pride in every tone of his voice.

"Oh, dearie," said Milly as she clasped Phoebe's hand, "we couldn't come without them—everything happened wrong. I know it's awful and I ought to take them right back now and—"

"David Kildare," said Phoebe as she divined in an instant the whole situation, "I love—I love you for doing it," and she sank on her knees by Caroline. Mistake let go the chain and bobbed forward to bestow a moist kiss on this, his friend of long standing; and as he chuckled and snuggled his little nose under her white chin Phoebe's echo was a sigh of such absolute rapture that the whole circle shouted with glee.

And late as it was dinner was announced three times before the host or the guests could be persuaded to think of food. And not until David's bed was made ready for the little guests did they begin to make their way into the dining-room. It was Andrew who finally insisted on carrying the babes away and tucking them in—only Caroline went with him with Little Sister in her arms and laid her gently on the pillow. She refused to lift her eyes to him for so much as a half-second until he drew her chair from the table for her; but then her shy glance was deep with innocent tenderness.

"Now," said the major as they settled laughingly into their places, "everybody's glass high to the silent guests!" And they drank his toast with enthusiasm.

"And," added David Kildare as he set down his glass, "they needn't be 'silent guests' unless it suits them. When they want to rough-house they know Uncle David's is the place to come to do it in."

"But let's hope they won't want to, David," laughed Milly, radiant with excitement.

"I tell you what let's do," said the enlivened Hobson from the coveted seat next Caroline Darrah Brown, "let's all give them hard sleeping suggestions, all at the same time.... Maybe they won't wake up for a week."

"Andrew," said Mrs. Buchanan as she looked with delight in his direction, "these are delicious things you and David have to eat. I am so glad you are well again and can enjoy them."

"Better go slow, Andy," called David from down the table. "Sure you don't need a raw egg? Phoebe has a couple up her sleeve here she can lend you. The major has persuaded her to take a bit of duck and some asparagus and a brandied peach and—"

"David Kildare," said Phoebe in a coolly dangerous voice, "I will get even with you for that if it takes me a week. This is the first thing I have had to eat since meal before last and I lost two and a half pounds last week. So I'll see that you—"

"Please, please, Phoebe, I'll be good! Just let me off this time. I'm giddy from looking at you!" And before a delighted audience David Kildare abased himself.

"Anyway, I've got news to relate," he hastened to offer by way of propitiation. "What do you think has happened to Andrew? I didn't promise not to tell," he drawled, prolonging the agony to its limit.

"Hurry, David, do!" exclaimed Phoebe with suspended fork. Caroline leaned forward eagerly, while Andrew began a laughing protest.

"It's only that Hetherton is going to put the great Mainwright on in Andy's new play in the fall—letter came to-day. Now, doesn't he shove his pen to some form—some?" he demanded as he beamed upon his friend with the greatest pride.

"Oh," said Caroline Darrah, "Mainwright is great enough to do it—almost!"

A pulse of joy shot through Andrew as her excited eyes gleamed into his. Of them all she and the major only had read his play and could congratulate him really. He had turned to her instantly when David had made his announcement, and she had answered him as instantly with her delight.

"And Cousin Andy," asked Polly who sat next to him, "will I have to cry at the third act? Please don't make me, it's so unbecoming. Why can't people do all the wonderful things they do in plays without being so mussy?"

"Child," jeered David Kildare as they all laughed, "don't you know a heart-throb when you're up against it—er—beg pardon—I mean to say that plays are sold at so much a sob. Seems to me you get wise very slowly." Polly pouted and young Boston who sat next her went red up to his hair.

"Better let me look over the contracts for you, Andrew," said Tom Cantrell with friendly interest in his shrewd eyes. If the material was all Tom had to offer his friends he did that with generosity and sincerity.

So until the roses fell into softly wilting heaps and the champagne broke in the glasses they sat and talked and laughed. Pitched battles raged up and down the table and there were perfect whirlpools of argument and protestation. Phoebe was her most brilliant self and her laughter rang out rich and joyous at the slightest provocation. The major delighted in a give and take encounter with her and their wit drew sparks from every direction.

"No, Major," she said as the girls rose with Mrs. Buchanan after the last toast had been drunk, "toast my wit, toast my courage, toast my loyalty, but my beauty—ah, aren't women learning not to use it as an asset?"

As she spoke she stretched out one white hand and bare rounded arm to him in entreaty. Phoebe was more lovely than she knew as she flung her challenge into the camp of her friends and they all felt the call in her dauntless dawn-gray eyes. Her unconsciousness amounted to a positive audacity.

"Phoebe," answered the major as he rose and stood beside her chair, "all those things stir at times our cosmic consciousness, but beauty is the bouquet to the woman-wine—and *you* can't help it!"

"How do you old fellows down at the bivouac really feel about this conduit business, Major," said Tom Cantrell as he moved his chair close around by the major's after the last swish and rustle had left the men alone in the dining-room for a few moments. "Just a question starts father fire-eating, so I thought I would ask you to put me next. It's up in the city council."

"Tom," answered the major as he blew a ring of smoke between himself and the shrewd eyes, "what on earth have a lot of broken-down old Confederate soldiers got to do with the management of the affairs of the city? You young men are to attend to that—give us a seat in the sun and our pipes—of peace."

"Oh, hang, Major! Look at the way you old fellows swung that gas contract in the council. You 'sit in the sun' all right but they all know that the bivouac pulls the plurality vote in this city when it chooses—and they jump when you speak. What are you going to do about this conduit?"

"Is it pressing? Not much being said about it."

"That's it—they want to make it a sneak in. Mayor Potts is pushing hard and we know he's just the judge's catspaw. Judge Taylor owns the city council since that last election and I believe he has bought the board of public works outright. The conduit is just a whisky ring scheme to hand out jobs before the judge's election. They have got to keep the criminal court fixed, Major, for this town is running wide open day and night—with prohibition voted six months ago. They've got to keep Taylor on the bench. What do you say?"

"Well," answered the major, beetling his brows over his keen eyes, "I suppose there is no doubt that Taylor is machine-made. He's the real blind tiger, and Potts is his striped kitten. I understand he 'lost' four-fifths of the 'open' indictments that the grand jury 'found' on their last sitting. The whisky men are going to sell as long as the criminal court protects them, of course. Let's let them cut that conduit deeper into the public mind before they begin on the streets."

"I'm looking for a nasty show-down for this town before long, Major, if there are men enough in it to call the machine."

"Tom," answered the major as he blew a last ring from his cigar, "a town is in a rotten fix when the criminal court is a mockery. Let's go interrupt the women's dimity talk."

And it was quite an hour later that Milly decided in an alarmed hurry that she and the babies must take their immediate departure. David maneuvered manfully to send them home in his car and to have Phoebe wait and let him take her home later—alone. But Phoebe insisted upon going with Milly and Billy Bob and the youngsters, and the reflection that the distance from the unfashionable quarter inhabited by the little family, back to Phoebe's down-town apartment was very short, depressed him to the point of defiance—almost.

However, he packed them all in and then as skilfully unpacked them at the door of their little home. He carried up the twins and even remained a moment to help in their unswathing before he descended to the waiting car and Phoebe. As he gave the word and swung in beside her, David Kildare heaved a deep and rapturous sigh. It was so much to the good to have her to himself for the short whirl through the desolated winter streets. It was a situation to be made the most of for it came very seldom.

He turned to speak to her in the half light and found her curled up in the corner with her soft cheek resting against the cushions. Her attitude was one of utter weariness, but she smiled without opening her eyes as she nestled closer against the rough leather.

"Tired, peach-bud?" he asked softly. One of the gifts of the high gods to David Kildare was a voice with a timbre suitable to the utmost tenderness, when the occasion required.

"Yes," answered Phoebe drowsily, "but so happy! It was all lovely, David." Her pink-palmed hand lay relaxed on her knee. David lifted it cautiously in both his strong warm ones and bent over it, his heart ahammer with trepidation. For as a general thing neither the environment nor his mood had much influence in the softening way on Phoebe's cool aloofness, but this once some sympathetic chord must have vibrated in her heart for she clasped her fingers around his and received the caress on their pink tips with opening eyes that smiled with a hint of tenderness.

"David," she said with a low laugh, "I'm too tired to be stern with you tonight, but I'll hold you responsible to-morrow—for everything. Here we are; do see if that red-headed devil is sitting on the door-step and tell him that there is—no—more copy—if I *am* a half-column short. And, David," she drew their clasped hands nearer and laid her free one over both his as the car drew up to the curb, "you—are—a—dear! Here's my key in my muff. To-morrow at five? I don't know—you will have to phone me. Good night, and thank you—dear. Yes—good night again!"

CHAPTER VI

THE BRIDGE OF DREAMS

"And then, Major, hell broke loose! Dave stood up and—" Tom Cantrell's eyes snapped and he slashed with his crop at the bright andirons that held the flamed logs.

"No, Major, it wasn't hell that broke up, it was something inside me. I felt it smash. For a moment I didn't grasp what Taylor was saying. It sounded so like the ravings of an insane phonograph that I was for being amused, but when I found that he was actually advising the mayor to refuse our committee the use of the hay market for a bivouac during the Confederate reunion, I just got up and took his speech and fed it to him raw. I saw red with a touch of purple and I didn't know I was on my feet and—"

"Major," interrupted Andrew Sevier, his eyes bright as those of Kildare and his quiet voice under perfect control, "Judge Taylor's exact words were that it seemed inadvisable to turn over property belonging to the city for the use of parties that could in no way be held responsible. He elucidated his excuse by saying that the Confederate soldiers were so old now that they were better off at home than parading the streets and inciting rebellious feelings in the children, throwing the city into confusion by their disorderly conduct and—"

"That's all he said, Major, that's all. I was on my feet then and all that needs to be said and done to him was said and done right there. I said it and Phoebe and Mrs. Peyton Kendrick did it as they walked right past him and out of the chamber of commerce hall of committees while he was trying to answer me. That broke up the meeting and he can't be found this morning. Cap has had Tom looking for him. I think when we find him we will have a few more words of remonstrance with him!" said Dave quietly. And he stood straight and tall before the major, and as he threw back his head he was most commanding. There was an expression of power in the face of David Kildare that the major had never seen there before.

He balanced his glasses in his hands a moment and looked keenly at the four young men lined up before him. They made a very forceful typification of the new order of things and were rather magnificent in their defense of the old. The major's voice tightened in his throat before he could say what they were waiting to hear.

"Boys," he said, and his old face lit with one of its rare smiles, "there were live sparks in these gray ashes—or we could not have bred you. I'm thinking you, yourselves, justify the existence of us old Johnnies and give us a clear title to live a little while longer, reunite once a year, sing the old songs, speechify, parade, bivouac a few more times together—and be as disorderly as we damn please, in this or any other city's hay market. Tom, telephone Cap to go straight to the bivouac headquarters and have them get ready to get out a special edition of the *Gray Picket*. If reports of this matter are sent out over the South without immediate and drastic refutations there will be a conflagration of thousands of old fire-eaters. They will never live through the strain. Andrew, take David up to your rooms, send for a stenographer and get together as much of that David Kildare speech as you can. Hobson, get hold of the stenographer of the city council and get his report of both Taylor's and Potts' speeches. Choke it out of him for I suspect they have both attempted to have them destroyed."

"Don't you see, Major, don't you see, he tried to make a play to the masses of protecting the city's property and the city's law and order, but he jumped into a hornet's nest? We managed to keep it all out of the morning paper but something is sure to creep in. Hadn't we better have a conference with the editors?" Tom was a solid quantity to be reckoned with in a stress that called for keenness of judgment rather than emotion.

"Ask them for a conference in the editorial rooms of the *Gray Picket* at two-thirty, Tom," answered the major. "In the meantime I'll draft an editorial for the special edition. We must come out with it in the morning at all odds."

In a few moments the echo of their steps over the polished floors and the ring of their voices had died away and the major was once more alone in his quiet library. He laid aside his books and drew his chair up to the table and began to make preparations for his editorial utterances. His rampant grizzled forelock stood straight up and his jaws were squared and grim. He paused and was in the act of calling Jeff to summon Phoebe over the wire when the curtains parted and she stood on the threshold. The major never failed to experience a glow of pride when Phoebe appeared before him suddenly. She was a very clear-eyed, alert, poised individuality, with the freshness of the early morning breezes about her.

"My dear," he said without any kind of preliminary greeting, "what do you make of the encounter between David Kildare and Julge Taylor? The boys have been here, but I want your account of it before I begin to take action in the matter."

"It was the most dastardly thing I ever heard, Major," said Phoebe quietly with a deep note in her voice. "For one moment I sat stunned. The long line of veterans as I saw them last year at the reunion, old and gray, limping some of them, but glory in their bright faces, some of them singing and laughing, came back to me. I thought my heart would burst at the insult to them and to—us, their children. But when David rose from his chair beside me I drew a long breath. I wish you could have heard him and seen him. He was stately and courteous—and he said it *all*. He voiced the love and the reverence that is in all our hearts for them. It was a very dignified forceful speech—and *David* made it!" Phoebe stood close against the table and for a moment veiled her tear-starred eyes from the major's keen glance.

"Phoebe," he said after a moment's silence, "I sometimes think the world lacks a standard by which to measure some of her vaster products. Perhaps you and I have just explored the heart of David Kildare so far. But a heart as fine as his isn't going to pump fool blood into any man's brain—eh?"

"Sometimes and about some things, you do me a great injustice, Major," answered Phoebe slowly, with a serious look into the keen eyes bent upon hers. "Of all the 'glad crowd', as David calls us, I am the only woman who comes directly in contact with the struggling, working, hand-to-hand fight of life, and I can't help letting it affect me in my judgment of—of us. I can't forget it when—when I amuse myself or let David amuse me. I seem to belong with them and not in the life he would make for me; yet you know I care—but if you are going to get out that extra edition you must get to work. I will sit here and get up my one o'clock notes for the imp, and if you need me, tell me so."

The major bestowed a slow quizzical smile upon her and took up his pen. For an hour they both wrote rapidly with now a quick question from the major and a concise answer from Phoebe, or a short debate over the wording of one of his sentences or paragraphs. The editorial minds of the graybeard and the girl were of much the same quality and they had written together for many years. The major had gone far in the molding of Phoebe's keen wit.

"Why, here you are, Phoebe," exclaimed Mrs. Buchanan as she hurried into the room just as Phoebe was finishing some of her last paragraphs, "Caroline and I have been telephoning everywhere for you. Do come and motor out to the Country Club with us for lunch. David and Andrew left some partridges there yesterday as they came from hunting on Old Harpeth, to be grilled for us to-day. You are going out there to play bridge with Mrs. Shelby's guest from Charleston at three, so please come with us now!"

She was all eagerness and she rested one plump, persuasive little hand on Phoebe's arm. To Mrs. Matilda, any time that Phoebe could be persuaded to frolic was one of undimmed joy.

"Now, Mrs. Matilda," said the major, as he smiled at her with the expression of delight that her presence always called forth even in times of extreme strenuosity, "do leave Phoebe with me—I'm really a very lorn old man."

"Why, are you really lonely dear? Then Caroline and I won't think of going. We'll stay right here to lunch with you. I will go tell her and you put up your books and papers and we will bring our sewing and chat with you and Phoebe. It will be lovely."

"Matilda," answered the major hastily with real alarm in his eyes, "I insist that you unroll my strings to your apron as far as the Country Club this once. I capitulate—no man in the world ever had more attention than I have. Why, Phoebe knows that—"

"Indeed, indeed, he really doesn't want us, Mrs. Matilda. Let's leave him to his Immortals. I will be ready in a half-hour if I can write fast here. Tell Caroline Darrah to hunt me up a fresh veil and phone Mammy Kitty not to expect me home until— until midnight. Now while you dress I will write."

"Very well," answered Mrs. Buchanan, "if you are sure you don't need us, Major," and with a caress on his rampant lock she hurried away.

"You took an awful risk then, Major," said Phoebe with a twinkle in her eyes.

"I know it," answered the major. "I've been taking them for nearly forty years. It's added much to this affair between Mrs. Buchanan and me. Small excitements are all that are necessary to fan the true connubial flame. I didn't tell her about all this because I really hadn't the time. Tell her on the way out, for I expect there will be a rattle of musketry as soon as the dimity brigade hears the circumstances."

Then for a half-hour Phoebe and the major wrote rapidly until she gathered her sheets together and left them under his paper-weight to be delivered to the devil from the office.

She departed quietly, taking Mrs. Matilda and Caroline with her.

And for still another hour the major continued to push his pen rapidly across the paper, then he settled down to the business of reading and annotating his work.

For years Major Buchanan had been the editor of *the Gray Picket,* which went its way weekly into almost every home in the South. It was a quaint, bright little folio full of articles of interest to the old Johnnie Rebs scattered south of Mason and Dixon. As a general thing it radiated good cheer and a most patriotic spirit, but at times something would occur to stir the gray ashes from which would fly a crash of sparks. Then again the spirit of peace unutterable would reign in its columns. It was published for the most part to keep up the desire for the yearly Confederate reunions—those bivouacs of chosen spirits, the like of which could never have been before and can never be after. The major's pen was a trenchant one but reconstructed—in the main.

But the scene at the Country Club in the early afternoon was, according to the major's prediction, far from peaceful in tone; it was confusion confounded. Mrs. Peyton Kendrick was there and the card-tables were deserted as the players, matrons and maids, gathered around her and discussed excitedly the result of her "ways and means for the reunion" mission to the city council, the judge's insult and David Kildare's reply. They were every mother's daughter of them Dames of the Confederacy and their very lovely gowns were none the less their fighting clothes.

"And then," said Mrs. Payt, her cheeks pink with indignation, and the essence of belligerency in her excited eyes, "for a moment I sat petrified, *petrified* with cold rage, until David Kildare's speech began—there had never been a greater one delivered in the United States of America! He said—he said—oh, I don't know what he did say, but it was—"

"I just feel—" gasped Polly Farrell with a sob, "that I ought to get down on my knees to him. He's a hero—he's a—"

"Of course for a second I was surprised. I had never heard David Kildare speak about a—a serious matter before, but I could have expected it, for his father was a most brilliant lawyer, and his mother's father was our senator for twenty years and his uncle our ambassador to the court of—" and Mrs. Peyton's voice trailed off in the clamor.

"Well, I've always known that Cousin Dave was a great man. He ought to be the president or governor—or *something*. I would vote for him to-morrow—or that is, I would make some man—I don't know just who—do it!" And Polly's treble voice again took up the theme of David's praises.

"And think of the old soldiers," said Mrs. Buchanan with a catch in her breath. "It will hurt them so when they read it. They will think people are tired of them and that we don't want them to come here in the spring for the reunion. They are old and feeble and they have had so much to bear. It was cruel, *cruel*."

"And to think of not wanting the children to see them and know them and love them—and understand!" Milly's soft voice both broke and blazed.

"I'm going to cry—I'm doing it," sobbed Polly with her head on Phoebe's shoulder. "I wasn't but twelve when they met here last time and I followed all the parades and cried for three solid days. It was delicious. I'm not mad at any Yankee—I'm in love with a man from Boston and I'm—oh, please, don't anybody tell I said that! I may not be, I just think so because he is so good-looking and—"

"We must all go out to the Soldier's Home to-morrow, a large committee, and take every good thing we can think up and make. We must pay them so much attention that they will let us make a joke of it," said Mrs. Matilda thinking immediately of the old fellows who "sat in the sun"—waiting.

"Yes," answered Mrs. Peyton, "and we must go oftener. We want some more committees. It won't be many years—two were buried last week from the Home." There was a moment's silence and the sun streamed in across the deserted tables.

"Oh," murmured Caroline Darrah Brown with her eyes in a blaze, "I can't stand it, Phoebe. I never felt so before—I who have no right."

"Dear," said Phoebe with a quiet though intensely sad smile, "this is just an afterglow of what they must have felt in those awful times. Let's get them started at the game."

For just a moment longer Phoebe watched them in their heated discussion, then chose her time and her strong quiet voice commanded immediate attention.

"Girls," she said, and as she spoke she held out her hand to Mrs. Peyton Kendrick with an audacious little smile. Any woman from two to sixty likes to be called girl—audaciously as Phoebe did it. "Let's leave it all to the men. I think we can trust them to compel the judge to dine off his yesterday's remarks in tomorrow's papers. And then if we don't like the way they have settled with him we can have a gorgeous time telling them how much better they might have done it. Let's all play—everybody for the game!"

"And Phoebe!" called Mrs. Payt as she sat down at the table farthest in the corner. She spoke in a clear high-pitched voice that carried well over the rustle of settling gowns and shuffling cards: "We all intend after this to *see* that David Kildare gets what he wants—you understand?" A laugh rippled from every table but Phoebe was equal to the occasion.

"Why not, Mrs. Payt," she answered with the utmost cordiality. "And let's be sure and find something he really wants to present to him as a testimony of our esteem."

"Oh, Phoebe," trilled Polly, her emotions getting the better of her as she stood with score-card in hand waiting for the game to begin, "*I* can't keep from loving him myself and *you* treat him so mean!"

But a gale of merriment interrupted her outburst and a flutter of cards on the felts marked the first rounds of the hands. In a few minutes they were as absorbed as if nothing had happened to ruffle the depths; but in the pool of every woman's nature the deepest spot shelters the lost causes of life, and from it wells a tidal wave if stirred.

After a little while Caroline Darrah rose from a dummy and spoke in a low pleading tone to Polly, who had been watching her game, standing ready to score. Polly demurred, then consented and sat down while Caroline Darrah took her departure, quietly but fleetly, down the side steps.

She was muffled in her long furs and she swung her sable toque with its one drooping plume in her hand as she walked rapidly across the tennis-courts, cut through the beeches and came out on the bank of the brawling little Silver Fork Creek, that wound itself from over the ridge down through the club lands to the river. She stood by the sycamore for a moment listening delightedly to its chatter over the rocks, then climbed out on the huge old rock that jutted out from the bank and was entwined by the bleached roots of the tall tree. The strong winter sun had warmed the flat slab on the south side and, sinking down with a sigh of delight, she embraced her knees and bent over to gaze into the sparkling little waterfall that gushed across the foot of the boulder.

Then for a mystic half-hour she sat and let her eyes roam the blue Harpeth hills in the distance, that were naked and stark save for the lace traceries of their winter-robbed trees. As the sun sank a soft rose purple shot through the blue and the mists of the valley rose higher about the bared breasts of the old ridge.

And because of the stillness and beauty of the place and hour, Caroline Darrah began, as women will if the opportunity only so slightly invites them, to dream—until a crackle in a thicket opposite her perch distracted her attention and sent her head up with a little start. In a second she found herself looking across the chatty little stream straight into the eyes of Andrew Sevier, in which she found an expression of having come upon a treasure with distracting suddenness.

"Oh," she said to break the silence which seemed to be settling itself between them permanently, "I think I must have been dreaming and you crashed right in. I—I—"

"Are you sure you are not the dream itself—just come true?" demanded the poet in a matter-of-fact tone, as if he were asking the time of day or the trail home.

"I don't think I am, in fact I'm sure," she answered with a break in her curled lips. "The dream is a bridge, a beautiful bridge, and I've been seeing it grow for minutes and minutes. One end of it rests down there by that broken log—see where the little knoll swells up from the field?—and it stretches in a beautiful strong arch until it seems to cut across that broken-backed old hill in the distance. And then it falls across—but I don't know where to put the other end of it—the ground sinks so—it might wobble. I don't want my bridge to wobble."

Her tone was expressive of a real distress as she looked at him in appealing confusion. And in his eyes she found the dawn of an amused wonder, almost consternation. Slowly over his face there spread a deep flush and his lips were indrawn with a quick breath.

"Wait a minute, I'll show you," he said in almost an undertone. He swung himself across the creek on a couple of stones, climbed up the boulder and seated himself at her side. Then he drew a sketch-book from his pocket and spread it open on the slab before them.

There it was—the dream bridge! It rose in a fine strong curve from the little knoll, spanned across the distant ridge and fell to the opposite bank on to a broad support that braced itself against a rock ledge. It was as fine a perspective sketch as ever came from the pencil of an enthusiastic young Beaux Arts.

"Yes," she said with a delighted sigh that was like the slide of the water over smooth pebbles, "yes, that is what I want it to be, only I couldn't seem to see how it would rest right away. It is just as I dreamed it and,"—then she looked at him with startled jeweled eyes. "Where did I see it—where did you— what does it mean?" she demanded, and the flush that rose up to the waves of her hair was the reflection of the one that had stained his face before he came across the stream. "I think I'm frightened," she added with a little nervous laugh.

"Please don't be—because I am, too," he answered. And instinctively, like two children, they drew close together. They both gazed at the specter sketch spread before them and drew still nearer to each other.

"I have been planning it for days," he said in almost a whisper. Her small pink ear was very near his lips and his breath agitated two little gold tendrils that blew across it. "I want to build it before I go away, it is needed here for the hunting. I came out and made the sketch from right here an hour ago. I came back—I must have come back to have it—verified." He laughed softly, and for just a second his fingers rested against hers on the edge of the sketch.

"I'm still frightened," she said, but a tippy little smile coaxed at the corners of her mouth. She turned her face away from his eyes that had grown—disturbing.

"I'm not," he announced boldly. "Beautiful wild things are flying loose all over the world and why shouldn't we capture one for ourselves. Do you mind—please don't!"

"I don't think I do," she answered, and her lashes swept her cheeks as she lifted the sketch-book to her knees. "Only suppose I was to dream—some of your—other work—some day? I don't want to build your bridges—but I might want to—write some of your poems. Hadn't you better do something to stop me right now?" The smile had come to stay and peeped roguishly out at him from beneath her lashes.

"No," he answered calmly, "if you want my dreams—they are yours."

"Oh," she said as she rose to her feet and looked down at him wistfully, "your beautiful, beautiful dreams! Ever since that afternoon I have gone over and over the lines you read me. The one about the 'brotherhood of our heart's desires' keeps me from being lonely. I think—I think I went to sleep saying it to myself last night and—"

It couldn't go on any longer—as Andrew rose to his feet he gathered together any stray wreckage of wits that was within his reach and managed, by not looking directly at her, to say in a rational, elderly, friendly tone, slightly tinged with the scientific:

"My dear child, and that's why you built my bridge for me to-day. You put yourself into mental accord with me by the use of my jingle last night and fell asleep having hypnotized yourself with it. Things wilder than fancies are facts these days, written in large volumes by extremely erudite old gentlemen and we believe them because we must. This is a simple case, with a well-known scientific name and—"

"But," interrupted Caroline Darrah, and as she stood away from him against the dim hills, her slender figure seemed poised as if for flight, and a hurt young seriousness was in her lifted purple eyes: "I don't want it to be a 'simple case' with any scientific—" and just here a merry call interrupted her from up-stream.

Phoebe and Polly had come to summon her back to the club; tea was on the brew. With the intensest hospitality they invited Andrew to come, too. But he declined with what grace he could and made his way through the tangle down-stream as they walked back under the beeches.

Thus a very bitter thing had come to Andrew Sevier—and sweet as the pulse of heaven. In his hand he had seen a sensitive flower unfold to its very heart of flame.

"Never let her know," he prayed, "never let her know."

CHAPTER VII

STRANGE WILD THINGS

"Phoebe," said David Kildare as he seated himself on the corner of the table just across from where Phoebe sat in Major Buchanan's chair writing up her one o'clock notes, "what is there about me that makes people think they must make me judge of the criminal court of this county? Do I look job-hungry so as to notice it?"

"No," answered Phoebe as she folded her last sheet and laid down her pencil, "that is one thing no one can accuse you of, David. But your work down there has brought its results. They need you and are calling to you rather decisively I think. Any more delegations to-day?"

"Several. Susie Carrie Snow came with more Civic Improvements, rather short as to skirts and skimpy as to hats. They have fully decided that I am going to feed Mayor Potts out of my hand as Taylor does, and they want my influence to put up two more drinking fountains and three brass plates to mark the homes of the founders of the city, in return for their precious support. I promised; and they fell on my neck. That is, if *you* don't mind?" David edged a tentative inch or two nearer Phoebe who had rested her elbows on the table and her head on her hands as she looked up at him.

"I don't," she answered with a cruel smile. Then she asked, with an unconcerned glance over the top of his head, "Did you hear from the United Charities?"

"Well, yes, some," returned David with an open countenance, no suspicion of a trap in even the flicker of an eyelash. "They sent Mrs. Cherry. Blooming more every day isn't she, don't you think? She didn't fall on my neck worth a cent though I had braced myself for the shock. She managed to convey the fact that the whole organization is for me just the same. It's some pumpkins to be a candidate. I'm for all there is in it—if at all."

"You aren't hesitating, David?" asked Phoebe as she rose and stood straight and tall beside him, her eyes on a level with his as he sat on the table. "Ah, David, you can if you will—will you? I know what it means to you," and Phoebe laid one hand on his shoulder as she looked him straight in the eyes, "for it will be work, *work* and fight like mad to put out the fire. You will have to fight honest—and they won't. But, David"—a little catch in her voice betrayed her as she entreated.

"Yes, dear," answered David as he laid his hand over the one on his shoulder and pressed it closer, "I sent in the announcement of my candidacy to the afternoon papers just as I came around here to see the major—and you. The fight is on and it is going to be harder than you realize, for there is so little time. Are you for me, girl?"

"If *I* fall on your neck it will make seven this morning. Aren't you satisfied?" And Phoebe drew her hand away from his, allowing, however, a regretful squeeze as he let it go.

"No, six if you would do it," answered David disconsolately, "I told you that Mrs. Cherry failed me."

"Yes," answered Phoebe as she lowered her eyes, "I know you told me." David Kildare was keen of wit but it takes a most extraordinary wisdom to fathom such a woman as Phoebe chose to be—out of business hours.

"Isn't it time for you to go to dress for the parade?" she asked quickly with apparent anxiety.

"No," answered David as he filled his tooled leather case from the major's jar of choice Seven Oaks heart-leaf—he had seen Phoebe's white fingers roll it to the proper fineness just the night before, "I'm all ready! Did you think I was going to wear a lace collar and a sash? Everything is in order and I only have to be there at two to start them off. Everybody is placed on the platform and everybody is satisfied. The unveiling will be at three-thirty. You are going out with Mrs. Matilda early, aren't you? I want you to see me come prancing up at the head of the mounted police. Won't you be proud of me?"

"Sometimes, really, I think you are the missing twin to little Billy Bob," answered Phoebe with a laugh, but in an instant her face became grave again. "I'm worried about Caroline Darrah," she said softly. "I found her crying last night after I had finished work. I was staying here with Mrs. Matilda for the night and I went into her room for a moment on the chance that she would be awake. She said she had wakened from an ugly dream—but I know she dreads this presentation, and I don't blame her. It was lovely of her to want to give the statue and plucky of her to come and do it—but it's in every way trying for her."

"And isn't she the darling child?" answered David Kildare, a tender smile coming into his eyes. "Plucky! Well I should say so! To come dragging old Peters Brown's money-bags down here just as soon as he croaked, with the express intention of opening up and passing us all our wads back. Could anything as—as pathetic ever have happened before?"

"No," answered Phoebe. Then she said slowly, tentatively, as she looked into David's eyes that were warm with friendliness for the inherited friend who had preempted a place in both their hearts: "And the one awful thing for which she can offer no reparation she knows nothing of. I pray she never knows!"

Maria Thompson Daviess

"Yes, but it is about to do him to the death. I sometimes wake and find him sitting over his papers at daybreak with burned-out eyes and as pale as a white horse in a fog."

"But why does it *have* to be that way? Andrew isn't bitter and it isn't her fault—she wasn't even born then. She doesn't even know."

"I think it's mostly the money," said David slowly. "If she were poor it would be all right to forgive her and take her, but a man couldn't very well marry his father's blood money. And he's suffering God knows. Here I've been counting for years on his getting love-tied at home, and to think it should be like this! Sometimes I wish she *did* know—she offers herself to him like a little child; and thinks she is only doing reverence to the poet. It's driving him mad, but he won't cut and run."

"And yet," said Phoebe, "it would kill her to know. She is so sensitive and she has just begun to be herself with us. She has had so few friends and she isn't like we are. Why, Polly Farrell could manage such a situation better than Caroline Darrah. She is so elemental that she is positively—primitive. I am frightened about it sometimes—I can only trust Andrew." As Phoebe spoke her eyes grew sad and her lips quivered.

"Dear heart," said David as he took both her hands in his, "it's just one of those fatal things that no man can see through; he can just be thankful that there's a God to handle 'em." There were times when David Kildare's voice held more of tenderness than Phoebe was calculated to withstand without heroic effort. It behooved her to exert the utmost at this moment in order that she might hold her own.

"It's making me thin," she ventured as she shook a little shower of tears off her black lashes and again smilingly regained control of her own hands, but displaying a slender blue-veined wrist for his sympathetic inspection.

"Help!" exclaimed David, taking possession of the wrist and

circling it with his thumb and forefinger. "Let me send for a crate of eggs and a case of the malt-milk! You poor starved peach-bud you, *why won't* you marry me and let me feed you? I'm going—"

"But you and the major both recommended 'lovers' troubles' to me, David," Phoebe hazarded.

"I only recommended *my* own special brand, remember," retorted David. "I won't have you ill! I'm going to see that you do as I say about your—"

"David Kildare," remarked the major from the door into the hall, "if you use that tone to the grand jury they will shut up every saloon in Hell's Half Acre. Hail the judge! My boy, my boy, I knew you'd line up when the time came—and the line!"

"Can I count on the full artillery of the *Gray Picket* brigade, Major?" demanded David with delight in his eyes as he returned the major's vigorous hand-shake.

"Hot shot, grape, canister and shrapnel, sir! Horses in lather, guns on the wheel and bayonets set. We'll bivouac in the camp of the enemy on the night of the election! We'll—"

"I don't believe you will want to lie down in the lair of the blind tiger as soon as that, Major," laugher Phoebe.

"Phoebe," answered the major, "politics makes strange bed-fellows. Mike O'Rourke, the boss of the democratic Irish, was around this morning hunting for David Kildare with the entire green grocer's vote in his pocket. He spoke of the boy as his own son."

"Good for old Mike!" laughed David. "It's not every boy who can boast an intimate friendship with his corner grocer from childhood up. It means a certain kind of—self-denial in the matter of apples and other temptations. I used to go to the point of an occasional errand for him. Those were the days,

Phoebe, when you sat on the front steps and played hollyhock dolls. Wish I'd kidnapped you then—when I could!"

"It would have saved us both lots of time—and trouble," answered Phoebe daringly from the protection of the major's presence.

"David, sir," said the major who had been busy settling himself in his chair and lighting his pipe during this exchange of pleasantries between David and Phoebe, to the like of which he was thoroughly accustomed, "this is going to be a fight to the ditches. I believe the whisky ring that controls this city to be the worst machine south of Mason and Dixon's. State-wide prohibition voted six months ago and every saloon in the town going full tilt night and day! They own the city council, the board of public works and the mayor, but none of that compares in seriousness to the debauching of our criminal courts. The grand jury is helpless if the judge dismisses every true bill they return—and Taylor does it every time if it is a whisky law indictment or pertaining thereto, and most of the bills are at least distantly pertaining. So there you have us bound and helpless—a disgrace to the nation, sir, and a reproach to good government!"

"Yes, Major, they've got us tied up some—but they forgot to gag us," answered David with a smile. "Your editorial in the *Gray Picket*, calling on me to run for criminal court judge, has been copied in every paper in the state and some of the large northern sheets. I am willing to make the try, Major. I've practised down there more than you'd think and it's rotten from the cellar steps to the lightning-rod. Big black buck is sent up for rioting down at Hein's Bucket of Blood dive—stand aside and forget about it—while some poor old kink is sent out to the pen for running into a flock of sleepy hens in the dark, 'unbeknownst' entirely. I defended six poor pick-ups last week myself, and I guess Taylor saw my blood was on the boil at the way he's running things. I'm ready to take a hand with him, but it will take some pretty busy doing around to beat the booze gang. Am I the man—do you feel sure?"

As David questioned the major his jaw squared itself determinedly. There was a rather forceful sort of man appearing under the nonchalant David whom his friends had known for years. A wild pride stirred in Phoebe to such an extent that she caught her breath while she waited for the major's reply.

"Yes, David," answered the major as he looked up at him with his keen old eagle eyes, "I think you are. You've had everything this nation can give you in the way of fighting blood from Cowpens to Bull Run, and when you speak in a body legislative your voice can be but an echo of the men who sired you, statesmen, most of them; so it is to you and your class we must look for clean government. It is your arraignment of the mayor and the judge on the hay-market question that has made every decent organization in the city look to you to begin the fight for a clean-up reorganization. They have all rallied to your support. Show your colors, boy, and, God willing, we will smash this machine to the last cog and get on a basis of honest government."

"Then here goes the hottest fight Davie knows how to put to them! And it's going to be an honest one. I'll go before the people of this city and promise them to enforce law and order, but I'll not *buy* a vote of a man of them. That I mean, and I hereby hand it out to you two representatives of the press. From now on 'not a dollar spent' is the word and I'm back of it to make it go." As he spoke, Kildare turned to Phoebe and looked at her as man to man with nothing in his voice but the cool note of determination. It was a cold dash for Phoebe but the reaction brought hot pride to her eyes.

"Yes, David," she answered, "you can and you will."

The determination in her voice matched that in his, and her eyes met his with a glance in which lay a new expression—not the old tolerant affection nor the guarded defense, but one with a quality of comradeship that steadied every nerve in his body. Some men get the like from some women—but not often.

"They will empty their pockets to fight you," the major continued thoughtfully. "But there is a deal of latent honesty in human nature, after all, that will answer the right appeal by the right man. A man calls a man; and ask a crook to come in on the straight proposition, two to one he'll step over the line before he stops himself. This is an independent candidacy— let's ask them all in, without reference to age, color or 'previous condition of servitude'—in the broadest sense."

"Yes, and with the other construction, too, perhaps. We'll ask in the darks—but they won't come. They'll vote with the jug crowd every time. No nig votes for Dave without the dollar and the small bottle. How many do they poll, anyway, do you suppose?"

"Less than a thousand I think. Not overwhelming! But in an independent race it might hold the balance of power. We'll devise means to appeal to them; we must keep up all the fences, you see. A man who doesn't see to his fences is a mighty poor proposition as a farmer and—"

"Hicks was here this morning, Major dear, to talk about that very thing," said Mrs. Matilda as she came in just in time to catch the last of the major's remark. "He says that ten hogs got through into the north pasture and rooted up acres of grass and if you don't get the new posts to repair the fence he can't answer for the damage done. He told you about it more than a month ago and—"

"David Kildare," said the major with an enigmatical smile, "what you need to see you through life is a wife. When a man mounts a high-horse aeroplane and goes sailing off, dimity is the best possible ballast. Consider the matter I beg of you— don't be obdurate."

"Why, of course David is going to marry some day," answered Mrs. Matilda as she beamed upon them. "A woman gets along nicely unmarried but it is cruel to a man. Major, Jeff is waiting to help you into your uniform. Do be careful, for it is mended to the last stitch now and I don't see how it is going to hold together many more times."

"Gray uniforms have held together a long time, Matilda," answered the major softly as he took his departure.

"And we must all hurry and have lunch," said Mrs. Buchanan. "Phoebe and I want to be there in plenty of time to see the parade arrive. It always gives me a thrill to see the major ride up at the head of his company. I've never got over it all these years."

"How 'bout that, Phoebe?" asked David, once more his daring insistent self. "Seems it wasn't so young in me after all to think you might thrill a few glads to see me come prancing up. Now, will you be good?"

And it was only a little over two hours later that the parade moved on its way from the public square to the park. A goodly show they made and an interesting one, the grizzled old war-dogs in their faded uniforms with faces aglow under their tattered caps. They trudged along under their ragged banners in hearty good will, with now a limp and now a halt and all of them entirely out of step with the enthusiastic young band in its natty uniform. They called to one another, chaffed the mounted officers, sang when the spirit moved them and acted in every way like boys who were off on the great lark of their lives.

All along the line of march there were crowds to see them and cheer them, with here and there a white-haired woman who waved her handkerchief and smiled at them through a rain of tears.

The major rode at the head of a small and straggling division of cavalry whose men ambled along and guyed one another about the management of their green livery horses who were inclined to bunch and go wild with the music.

A few pieces of heavy artillery lumbered by next, and just behind them came three huge motor-cars packed and jammed with the old fellows who were too feeble to keep up with the procession. They were most of them from the Soldiers' Home and in spite of empty coat sleeves and crutches they bobbed up and down and waved their caps with enthusiasm as cheer after cheer rose whenever they came into sight.

Andrew Sevier stood at his study window and watched them go past, marching to the conflicting tunes of *The Bonnie Blue Flag*, played by the head band, and *Dixie* by the following one. It was great to see them again after five years; and in such spirits! He felt a cheer rise to his lips and he wanted to open the window and give lusty vent to it—but a keen pain caught it in his throat.

Always before he had ridden with David at the head of the division of the Confederacy's Sons, but to-day he stood behind the window and watched them go past him! There were men in those ranks who had slept in the ditches with his father, and to whom he had felt that his presence would be a reminder of an exceeding bitterness. The had quietly fought the acceptance of the statue offered by the daughter of Peters Brown from the beginning, but the granddaughter of General Darrah, who had led them at Chickamauga, must needs command their acceptance of a memorial to him and her mother.

And they would all do her honor after the unveiling. Andrew could almost see old General Clopton stand with bared head and feel the thrill with which the audience would listen to what would be a tender tribute to the war women. A wave of passionate joy swelled up in his heart—he *wanted* them to cheer her and love her and adopt her! It was her baptism into her heritage! And he gloried in it.

Then across his joy came a curious stifling depression—he found himself listening as if some one had called him, called for help. The music was dying away in the distance and the cheers became fainter and fainter until their echo seemed almost a sob. Before he had time to realize what he did he descended the stair, crossed the street and let himself into the Buchanan house.

He stood just within the library door and listened again. A profound stillness seemed to beat through the deserted rooms—then he saw her! She sat with her arms outspread across the table and her head bent upon a pile of papers. She was tensely still as if waiting for something to sound around her.

"Caroline!" It was the first time he had called her by her name and though the others had done it from the first, she had never seemed to notice his more formal address. It was beyond him to keep the tenderness that swept through every nerve out of his voice entirely.

"Yes," she answered as she raised her head and looked at him, her eyes shining dark in her white face, "I know I'm a coward—did you come back to make me go? I thought they might not miss me until it was too late to come for me. I didn't think—I—could stand it—please—please!"

"You needn't go at all, dear," he said as he took the cold hands in his and unclasped the wrung fingers. "Why didn't you tell them? They wouldn't have insisted on your going."

"I—I couldn't! I just could not say what I felt to—to—*them*. I wanted to come—the statue suggested itself—for her. I ought to have given it and gone back—back to my own life. I don't belong—there is something between them all and me. They love me and try to make me forget it and—"

"But, don't you see, child, that's just it? They love you so they hold you against all the other life you have had before. We're a strong love people down here—we claim our own!" A note in his voice brought Andrew to his senses. He let her hands slip from his and went around the table and sat down opposite to her. "And so you ran away and hid?" He smiled at her reassuringly.

"Yes. I knew I ought not to—then I heard the music and I couldn't look or listen. I—why, where did you come from? I thought you were in the parade with David. I felt—if you knew you would understand. I wished that I had asked you— had told you that I couldn't go. Did you come back for me?"

"No," answered Andrew with a prayer in his heart for words to cover facts from the clear eyes fixed on his—clear, comforted young eyes that looked right down to the rock bed of his soul. "You see the old boys rather upset me, too. I have been away so long—and so many of them are missing. I'm just a coward, too—'birds of a feather'—take me under your wing, will you?"

"I believe one of those 'strange wild things' has been flying around in the atmosphere and has taken possession of us again," said Caroline Darrah slowly, never taking her eyes from his. "I don't know why I know, but I do, that you came to comfort me. I was thinking about you and wishing I could tell you. Now in just this minute you've made me see that I have a right to all of you. I'm never going to be unhappy about it any more. After this I'm going to belong as hard as ever I can."

Something crashed in every vein in Andrew Sevier's body, lilted in his heart, beat in his throat and sparkled in his eyes. He sprang to his feet and held out his hand to her.

"Then come on and be adopted," he said. "I shall order the electric, and you get into your hat and coat. We can skirt the park and come in at the side of the Temple back of the platform so that you can slip into place before one-half of the sky-rockets of oratory have been exploded. Will you come?"

"Will you stay with me—right by me?" she asked, timidity and courage at war in her voice.

"Yes," he answered slowly, "I'll stay by you as long as you want me—if I can."

"And that," said Caroline Darrah Brown as she turned at the door and looked straight at him with a heavenly blush mounting in her cheeks, the tenderness of the ages curling her lips and the innocence of all of six years in her eyes, "will be always!" With which she disappeared instantly beyond the rose damask hangings.

And so when the ceremonies in the park were over and Caroline stood to clasp hands with each of the clamorous gray squad, Andrew Sevier waited just behind her and he met one after another of the sharp glances shot at him from under grizzled brows with a dignity that quieted even the grimmest old fire-eater.

And there are strange wild things that take hold on the lives of men—vital forces against which one can but beat helpless wings of mortal spirit.

CHAPTER VIII

THE SPELL AND ITS WEAVING

And after the confusion, the distress and the joy of the afternoon out in the park when she and her gift had been accepted and acclaimed, there came days full of deep and perfect peace to Caroline Darrah Brown.

Long, strenuously delightful mornings she spent with Tempie in the excitements of completing her most comprehensive culinary education and the amount of badinage she exchanged upon the subject with David Kildare occupied many of his unemployed minutes. His demands for the most intricate and soul-trying concoctions she took a perfect joy in meeting and his enthusiasm stimulated her to the attempting of the most difficult feats.

His campaign was on with full force and his days were busy ones, but he managed to drop into the kitchen at any time when he deemed it at all certain that he would find her there and was always fully rewarded.

He often found Andrew Sevier in the library in consultation with the major over the management of the delicate points in the campaign and occasionally brought him into Tempie's kingdom with him. And Caroline laughed and blushed and explained it all to them with the most beautiful solicitude, Tempie looking on positively bridling with pride.

And there were other mornings when she took her sewing and crept in the library to work, while the major and Andrew held consultation over the affairs of the present or absent David.

The whisky ring had purchased one of the morning papers, which had hitherto borne a reputation for extreme conservatism, and had it appear each morning with brilliant, carefully modulated arguments for the machine; doctored statistics and brought allegations impossible to be investigated in so short a time.

And all of every afternoon and evening Andrew Sevier sat at an editorial desk down at the office of the reform journal and pumped hot shot through their flimsy though plausible arguments. His blood was up and his pen more than a match for any in the state, so he often sat most of the night writing, reviewing and meeting issue after issue. The editor-in-chief, whose heart was in making a success of the campaign by which his paper would easily become the leading morning paper, gave him full rein, aided and abetted him by his wide knowledge of all the conditions and pointed out with unerring judgment the sore spots on the hide of the enemy at which to send the gadfly of investigation.

So each day while Andrew and the major went carefully over possibilities to be developed by and against the enemy, Caroline listened with absorbed interest. Now and then she would ask a question which delighted them both with its ingenuousness, but for the most part she was busily silent.

And in the exquisiteness of her innocence she was weaving the spell of the centuries with the stitches in her long seams. There are yet left in the world a few of the elemental women whose natures are what they were originally instituted and Caroline Darrah was unfolding her predestined self as naturally as a flower unfolds in the warmth of the spring sunshine. The cooking for David and Andrew, the sewing for busy Phoebe, the tactfully daughterly attentions to the major and Mrs. Matilda were all avenues for the outpouring of the maturing woman within, and powerless in his enchantment, Andrew Sevier was swept along on the tide of her tenderness.

One day she had picked up his heavy gray gloves from the table and tightened the buttons, listening all the while to an absorbing account of a counter-move he was planning for the next day's editorial, and then had been delightfully confused and distressed by his gratitude. The little scene had sent him to the bare fields to fight for hours.

The major fairly gloried in her knowledge of the arrangement of his library and delighted her with quick requests for his books during the most absorbing moments of their discussions.

And again the observation that the spell was not being woven for him alone went far to the undoing of Andrew Sevier. Her interest in the affairs of David Kildare disturbed him not at all, but her sympathetic and absorbed attention to a bad-luck tale with which Hobson Capers reported to the major one morning when she sat with them, had sent him home in a most depressed state of mind, and the picture of her troubled eyes raised to Hobson's as he recounted the details of the wrenched shoulder of his favorite horse, followed him through the day with tormenting displeasure, though the offer of a cut-glass bottle full of a delightfully scented lotion for the amelioration of the suffering animal brought the semblance of a grin. And Hob, the brute, had gone away with it in his pocket, accompanied by explicit directions as to its application by means of a soft bit of flannel the size of a pocket handkerchief, also provided. Andrew Sevier had a vision of the bottle and the rag being installed in the most holy of holies in the apartments of Hobson Capers and experienced a sweeping smashing rage thereat.

A day or two later a scene he had witnessed in the kitchen, in which Caroline and Tempie hung anxiously over a simmering pan of lemon juice, sugar, rye whisky and peppermint which, when it arrived at the proper sirupy condition, was to be administered as a soothing potion to the hoarse throat of Peyton Kendrick, who perched croaking on a chair close by, drove him to seeking comfort from Phoebe much to her apparent amusement but secret perturbation, for Phoebe both comprehended and feared the situation.

And thus there is also much of the primitive left in the heart of the modern man on which the elemental forces work.

Then the day for the election came nearer and nearer by what seemed fleeting hours. The whole city was thoroughly aroused and fighting hard under one banner or the other. As the last week drew to a close and left only the few days of the following week for a round-up of the forces before the Wednesday election, the men all became absorbed to the point of oblivion to everything save the speculation as to how the race would go. But it was not in the nature of David Kildare to be held against the grindstone of serious endeavor too long at a time, and in the midst of the turmoil he proceeded to plot for a brief and exciting relaxation for himself and his strenuous friends, and he chose Saturday for the accomplishment thereof.

The morning dawned in a fluff of gray fog that hung low down over the avenue, though the sun showed signs of soon piercing the gloom. The clash and clatter of the city was fast approaching a noonday roar but still Phoebe slept in the room which adjoined that of Caroline Darrah Brown.

Caroline cautiously opened the door and stole in gently to the side of the bed, then paused and looked down with delight. Phoebe, asleep, was a thing calculated to bring delight to any beholder. The brilliant, casual, insouciant, worldly Phoebe had gone out on a dream-hunt and a delicious curled-up flower lay in her place, with turned lashes dipping against soft tinted cheeks. Her head rested on one bare white arm and one hand curled under her daintily molded chin. Caroline caught her breath—this was a pathetic Phoebe when one thought of the most times Phoebe, cool, self-reliant—perforce!

"The darling," she whispered to herself as she slipped to her knees by the low bed, "I can't bear to wake her, but I'm afraid not to; it's an hour late already. Dear!" She slipped her arm under the glossy head and pressed a little kiss on the dimple over the northeast corner of the warm lips.

Phoebe's gray eyes smiled themselves open for a fraction of a second, then she nestled to Caroline's shoulder and calmly drifted off again in pursuit of the dream.

"Dearie," Caroline begged, "it's after ten!"

Phoebe sighed, nestled closer and drifted again. Caroline settled herself against the pillows and pressed her cheek against the thick black braid that curled across the sleeper's bare shoulder. She was incapable of another combat with the sleep-god and decided to wait. Besides, the awake Phoebe was busy—and elusive—not given to bestowing or receiving aught save the most fleeting caresses. So for a few moments Caroline Darrah's arms held her hungrily.

"Be-autiful," came in a sleepy voice from against her arm, "is the water cold?"

"Awful this morning," answered Caroline tightening her arms. "Just a little hot, Phoebe, please! I'll tell Annette."

"No," answered Phoebe, as with a whirl of the covers she sat up and took her knees into her embrace. "No, sweetie, in I go! The colder the better after I'm in. How grand and Burne-Jonesy you look in that linen pinafore—indulging in the life domestic? I think I catch a whiff of your culinary atmosphere—and, oh, I—am so—hungry."

"Tempie has a dear little plump bird for you and some waffles and an omelet. Let me have Annette bring them to you here! Please, Phoebe, please!"

"Caroline Darrah Brown," said Phoebe in a tragic voice, "do

you know I gained a pound and a quarter last week and that makes me three and a half pounds past the danger-mark? Two raw eggs and an orange is all I can have this morning. I'm going to cry, I think!"

"No," answered Caroline Darrah positively, "you are going to eat that bird and the omelet. You may substitute dry toast for the waffle if Tempie will let you. She's angry, and I'm in trouble. She won't use that recipe I got from your Mammy Kitty to make the cake I promised David Kildare for tea. She says she and her family have been making Buchanan cake ever since there was any cake and she is not going to begin now making Donelson mixtures. I think I hurt her feelings. What must I do?"

"Let her alone, she has the right of it and the cake is sure to be just as good," laughed Phoebe.

"But I promised him it should be just like the one you gave us the other afternoon, only with the icing and nuts thicker than the cake," answered Caroline in real distress. "He says that Mr. Sevier likes it that way, too," she added ingenuously.

"Caroline Darrah, you spoil those men to the most outrageous extent. It's like David to want his icing and nuts thicker than the cake; he always does—and gets it, but it isn't good for him." As Phoebe spoke she smiled at Caroline Darrah indulgently.

"I can't help it, Phoebe," she answered with the rose wave mounting under her eyes. "I'm stupid—I don't know how to manage them. I'm just—fond of them."

For a second Phoebe regarded her from under veiled eyes, then said guardedly, "Doesn't that give them rather the advantage to start with—if you let them find it out?"

"Yes," answered Caroline as she pressed her cheek against Phoebe's arm, "I know it does but I can't help it. I have to trust to them to understand."

For a moment Phoebe was silent and across her mind there flashed David's description of a man who sat into the gray dawn fighting his battle—his own and hers—a man who wouldn't run!

"Perhaps that's the best way after all, dearie," she said as she prepared to slip out of bed. "Only it takes the exceptional woman to get results from your method. It ought to work with David; others don't seem to!"

"Phoebe, Phoebe—why—why?" and Caroline caught and held Phoebe for a few seconds. "Don't you care at all?"

"Yes, child—a lot! Having admitted which I will betake myself to the plunge—leaving you to finish the cake for the precious thing." In a second Phoebe smiled back from the door:

"Just one little waffle, tell Tempie," she said. "And I'm due to make a lightning toilet if I get to that Woman's Guild meeting at eleven-thirty. Call the office for me and tell them not to send Freckles until one-thirty to-day. And, dearie, please call Polly and tell her to be sure and go to that meeting of the Daughters of the Colonies so she can tell me what happens. Tell her to get it all straight—names and all and I will phone her. And not to let them office or committee me just because I'm not there! You are a dear!"

Caroline smiled happily as she went back to the mixing of the confection of affection to be administered to David with his tea as by request, and she laughed as she heard Phoebe's mighty splash.

And a half-hour later, during the discussion of the plump bird and the one crisp waffle, David Kildare whirled in, beaming with joy over his plans. In fact he failed to manage anything in the way of a formal greeting.

"Girls!" he exclaimed from the doorway, "the hunt is on for to-night! Everybody hurry up! Caroline, Mrs. Matilda wants you to motor out with her to the Forks to see about having Jeff and Tempie get ready for the supper cooking—barbecue, birdies and the hot potato! Milly and Billy Bob are going and Polly and that Boston lad of yours, Caroline—yours if you can hold him, which I don't think you can. And Mrs. Matilda says—"

"Stop," demanded Phoebe, "and tell us what you are talking about, David."

"I'm surprised at you, Phoebe, for being so dense," answered David with a delighted grin at having created a flurry. "Didn't you hear me tell Caroline Darrah Brown at least a week ago that possums and persimmons are ripe and that the first night after a rain and a fog we would all turn out and show her how to shake down a few? The whole glad push is going. Mrs. Matilda and I decided it an hour ago while you were still asleep. I've telephoned everybody—possums and persimmons wait for no man."

"How perfectly delightful," said Caroline with eyes agleam with enthusiasm. "Can everybody go?" David had failed to mention Andrew Sevier in his enumeration, an omission that she had instantly caught.

"Yes," answered David, "everybody that had engagements we asked the engagement to go, too. Even Andy is going to cut the poems for the lark! Thuse up a little, Phoebe, please—give us the smile! I'm backing you to shake down ten possums against anybody's possible five."

"I don't think that I can go," answered Phoebe quietly. "Mrs. Cherry has the president of the Federation of Women's Clubs staying with her and I'm going to dine there to-night to discuss the suffrage platform." There was a cool note in Phoebe's voice and a sudden seriousness had come into her expression.

"Now, Phoebe," answered David, looking down at her with the quickly concealed tenderness that always flashed up in his eyes when he spoke directly to her, "do you suppose for one minute that I hadn't fixed all that the first thing? Mrs. Cherry held back a bit but I rabbit-footed the old lady into being wild to go and then wheedled the correct hostess some; and there you are! Caroline is to send them out in her motor and I'm going to make Hob and Tom chase the possum in company of the merry widow and Mrs. Big Bug. Now give me a glad word!"

"I'll see," answered Phoebe. "I can let you know by two o'clock whether I can go," and as she spoke she gathered up her gloves and bag and settled her trim hat by a glance at the long mirror across the room.

"What—what did you say?" demanded David aghast in a second. "If you think for one minute that I'm going to stand for—"

"But you must remember that my business engagements must always be settled before I can make social ones—at two o'clock then! Good-by, Caroline, dear, such a comfy night under your care! I'm going to stop in the library to speak to the major and then on to the guild if any one calls. Here's to you both!" and she coolly tipped them a kiss from the ends of her fingers.

"Caroline," remarked David, "I reckon I must have giggled too loud in my cradle, and the Lord turned around and made Phoebe to settle my glee, don't you think?"

And as Caroline saw him depart with his usual smile and jest she little realized that a jagged wound ran across his blithe heart.

The David within was awakening and developing a highly sensitized nature, which caught Phoebe's note of disapproval, divined its reason and winced under the humiliation of its distrust. The old David would have laughed, chaffed her and gone his way rejoicing—the new David suffered, for a deeply-loved woman can inflict a wound on the inner man that throbs to the depths.

Across the hall Phoebe found the major at his table and, as usual, buried in his books. He was reading one and holding another open in his hand while his pen balanced itself over a page for a note. Phoebe hesitated on the threshold, loath to disturb his feast. But before she could retreat he glanced up and his smile flashed a welcome and an invitation to her, while his books fell together as he rose and held out his hands.

"My dear," he said, "I was just reading what Bob Browning says about a 'pearl and a girl'—and thinking of you when up I look to behold you."

"Thank you, and good morning, Major," returned Phoebe as a slow smile spread over her grave face. "I won't disturb you, for I've only a moment! This hunt to-night—it—it troubles me. Has David forgotten that he is to make a speech on the cutting of the conduit over in the sixteenth ward at half-past seven o'clock? It is one of his most important appointments and—"

"Phoebe," answered the major as he balanced his pen on one long lean finger, "do you suppose that women will ever learn that men could dispense with them entirely after their second year—if it wasn't for the loneliness? I see David Kildare failed to make a sufficiently full apron-string report to you this morning of his intentions for the day."

"Sometimes, Major, you are completely horrid," answered Phoebe with both a smile and a spark in her eyes, "but I do care—that is, I'm interested, and—"

"It seems to me," the major filled in the pause, "that you are a trifle short on a woman's long suit—patience. Now in the case of David Kildare, you don't want to give him one moment of tortoise speed but must keep him pacing with the hare entirely. Remember the result of that race?"

"But I want him to win—he must! I think—"

"Did you hear that speech he made to the motley and their friends last Monday night? That was as fine an interpretation of the ethics involved in the enforcement of law as I have ever heard or read—delivered to simple minds unversed in the science ethical. He landed hot shot into the very stronghold of the enemy and his audience saw his points. I find the mind of David Kildare rather well provisioned with the diverse ammunition needed in political warfare. The whisky ring is making a stand and fighting the inches of retreat. I believe it to be retreat!"

"But can it be, Major? Andrew says that money is pouring into the city, even from other states. They intend to buy the election, come what will. How can a gentleman fight such a thing with 'not a dollar spent' announcement?"

"Phoebe," said the major with the quick illumination of one of his challenging smiles, "you can generally depend on the Almighty to back the right man when he's fighting the right fight. Suppose you put up a little faith on the event—be something of a sporting character and back David to win. Backing thoughts help in the winnings they tell us these days."

"I have, Major—I am—I do, but this hunt to-night positively—positively frightens me. It seemed so—so regardless of consequences—so trivial and—and inconsequent that—" Phoebe paused and the major was astonished to see that she was veiling tears with her thick black lashes.

"Phoebe, child," he said as he bent over quickly and laid his hand on hers, "I ought to have answered you sooner. He is prepared to make the speech of his life tonight at seven-thirty, but at ten he joins his friends to hunt. Didn't you draw your conclusions hurriedly—and against David?"

In a second the tightness in Phoebe's throat relaxed and the tears flowed back to their source, only one little splash jeweled her cheek that had flamed into a blush of joy and contrition.

"Ah," she said softly as she drew a deep breath, "I am so glad—glad!... I must hurry, for I'm an hour late already. Good-by!"

"Good-by, and remember that faith is one of the by-products of affection. And I might add that the right kind of faith finds tactful ways of—of admission. Do you see?" And the major held her hand long enough to make Phoebe look into his kind eyes.

And from the ten minutes in the library of Major Buchanan the disciplining of the heart of Phoebe Donelson began and was carried on with utter relentlessness. The first castigation occurred when David failed to phone her at two o'clock, and a half-hour later Caroline Darrah called anxiously to know her decision and impart the information that David had arranged that she and Phoebe go out to the fork in her car with Mrs. Buchanan. Phoebe, to her own surprise, found that she intensely desired another arrangement that involved David and his small electric, but she received the blow with astonishing meekness and delighted Caroline with her enthusiastic acquiescence in the plans for the evening.

And so through the busy afternoon while David Kildare met committees, sent in reports and talked over plans, he also managed to sandwich in the settling of numerous little details that went to make good the night's sport. And it was all done in apparent high spirits but with an indignant pain in his usually glad heart.

Meanwhile Caroline Darrah, in a whirl of domestic excitement incident to the preparing of a hamper for the midnight lunch out on the ridge, which she had entreated Mrs. Matilda to leave entirely to her newly-acquired housewifery, stepped into the middle of the pool political and never knew it, in the innocence of her old-fashioned woman's heart.

"Miss Ca'line," ventured Jeff as he assisted her in packing the huge hamper that occupied the center of the dining-room table, "is Mister Dave sure 'pinted to be jedge of the criminal court—he ain't a-joking is he?"

"Why, no, indeed, Jeff," answered Caroline Darrah as she rolled sandwiches in oiled paper before putting them into a box. "What made you think that?"

"Well, it's a kinder poor white folksy job fer him, fooling with crap-shooting niggers and whisky soaks, but if he wants it he's got ter have it, hear me! And Miss Ca'line, some of us colored set has made up our minds that it's time fer us ter git out and dust ter help him. You see this here is a independent race and it's who gits the votes, no 'Publican er Dimocrat to it. That jest naterally turns the colored vote loose at the polls. And fer the most of the black fools it's who bids the mostes, I'm sorry ter say, as is the fact."

"But you know Mr. David has said from the first that he will not buy a vote. Will he have to lose—how many of the colored people are there—oh, Jeff, will he have to be beaten?" Caroline Darrah clasped a sandwich to the death in her hands and questioned the negro with the same faith that she would have used in questioning Major Buchanan.

"No, ma'am, he ain't going ter git nigger-beat if we can help it—us society colored set, you understand, Miss Ca'line." Jeff's manner was an interesting mixture of pomposity and deference.

"I don't quite understand, Jeff; you explain to me," answered Caroline Darrah in the kind and respectful voice that she always used to these family servants, which they understood perfectly and in which they took a huge delight.

"Well, it's jest this way, Miss Ca'line, they is sets in the colored folks jest like they is in the white folks. We is the *it* set, me and Tempie and Eph and all the fust family people. We's got our lawyers and dentists and a university and a ice-cream parlor with the swellest kinder soda fount in front. You heard how Mister David got that Country Club for us, didn't you? Well, he backed the rent notes of the soda fount, too—and he's jest naterly the fust set candidate fer anything he wants ter be."

"Isn't he just the kindest best man, Jeff?" asked Caroline Darrah, in her enthusiasm sacrificing a frosted muffin cake between her clasped hands.

"Yes'm, he am that fer a fact, and they can't no low-down whisky bum beat him fer jedge, neither—'specially ef they count on using niggers to do it with. You see the race am so mighty close, that all the booze bosses is a telling the niggers that they is got the 'ballunce uf power' as they calls it and it's up ter them ter elect a jedge fer whisky, the friend 'at'll let 'em drink it down. Why, they's got out a bottle of whisky as has on the label 'Your Colored Friend', and it's put up in clear glass and at the bottom you can see five new dimes a-shining. A nigger gits the bottle and the fifty cents ef he votes with them. Old Booze is flinging money right and left, fer if Mister David gits in he'll shore have ter git out."

"That is perfectly awful, Jeff!" exclaimed Caroline with horror-stricken eyes. "The poor people made to sell themselves that way—and the whole city to lose David, a good judge, because they can't know what they do. It is horrible and nobody can help it!"

"I ain't so sure about that, Miss Ca'line! Me and Tempie and Doctor Pike Johnson and the dentist and Bud Simms, the man what runs the Palms, have thought up a scheme ef we kin work it. You see they ain't a nigger from Black Bottom to Mount Nebo as wouldn't sell his soul ter git ter the Country Club and say he's been invited there. Now, we thought as how it would be a good plan ter give it out that we was going to have er David Kildare jedge celebration out there and have invertation tickets printed. Then we could go ter the polls and fight down any dollar bottle of whisky ever put up with one of them invites—every man ter bring a lady, and dancing down in a corner of the card. We'd scotch them by saying no 'lection, no dance, so they'll vote straight. Ain't that the swell scheme? It'll work if we can make it go."

"Jeff," she exclaimed, "that is a perfectly splendid idea! You must do it, for offering them fun will be no bribery like whisky and money—it will do them *good*." Sometimes it is just as well that a woman be not too well versed in the science logical.

"Yes'm, and I believe it will work—ef we jest had a barbecue to put down in the other corner opposite the dancing I know it would draw 'em, but ice-cream will be about all we can git fer the subscription money, and cold as it is ice-cream won't be no drawing card."

And there was no doubt that Jeff unfolded his plan to Caroline Darrah from pure love of sympathy and excitement and for no ulterior purpose, although it served to further his schemes as well as if he had been of a most wily turn of mind.

"Jeff," exclaimed Caroline Darrah excitedly, "how much would it take to have a barbecue and ice-cream and everything good to go with it and a big band of music and fireworks and—"

"Golly, Miss Ca'line, they will be most five hundred of 'em and the 'scription ain't but a little over fifty dollars. I'm counting on the dancing and the gitting-there ter draw 'em."

"We can't risk it," said Caroline. "I will give you two hundred and fifty dollars and you can let it be known that no such celebration ever was as the one his colored friends are going to give in honor of the election of Judge David Kildare—his united colored friends, Jeff, high and low."

"Miss Ca'line, I'm a-skeered to take it! Mister David, he's jest naterly—"

"Mr. David need never know about it. It is a subscription and you have collected it—advertise that fact. I'm one of his friends and I can subscribe even if I am white. You must take it, and get to work about it. Only four more days, remember, and we all must work for Mr. David; and too, Jeff, for those poor ignorant people who would commit the crime of letting themselves sell their votes." There was real concern for the endangered souls of the coons in Caroline's voice, and Jeff was duly impressed.

They both fell to work on the packing of the basket as Temple's voice was heard in the distance, for they knew she would express herself in no uncertain terms if she found the amount of work done unsatisfactory.

But when he departed, Jeff carried in his pocket a slip of paper about which it nearly scared him to death to think, and one of the money-bags of the late Peters Brown was eased by the extraction of a quarter thousand. Caroline was happy from a clear conscience and a virtuous feeling of having saved a crisis for a dependent and ignorant people. Which goes to show that a woman can put her finger into a political pie and draw it out without even a stain, while to touch that same confection ever so lightly would dye a man's hand blood red.

Maria Thompson Daviess

CHAPTER IX

PURSUING THE POSSUM

And as if in sympathy with the heart of the pursued possum, the thermometer began to fall in the afternoon and by night had established a clear, cold, windless condition of weather. The start for the Cliffs was to be made from the fork of the River Road, where cars, horses, traps and hampers were to be left with the servants, who by half past nine were already in an excited group around a blazing, dry oak fire, over which two score plump birds were ready to be roasted, attended by the autocratic Tempie. Jeff piled high with brush a huge log whose heart was being burned out for the baking of sundry potatoes, while the aroma from the barbecue pit was maddening to even a ten o'clock appetite, and no estimate could be made of what damage would be done after the midnight return from the trail of the wily tree fruit.

David Kildare as usual was M.F.H. and his voice rang out as clearly against the tall pines, while he welcomed the cars and traps full of excited hunters, as if he had not been speaking in a crowded hall for an hour or two.

Mrs. Cherry Lawrence arrived early, accompanied by the distinguished suffragist, who was as alert for sensations new as if she had been one of an exploration party into the heart of darkest Africa. They were attended by Tom and also the suave Hobson, who was all attentions but whose maneuvers in the direction of Caroline Darrah were pitiably fruitless. He was seconded in his attentions to the stranger by David with his most fascinating manner, and Mrs. Cherry sparkled and glowed at him with subdued witchery, while Tom sulked close at her side.

Polly and young Boston had trailed Mrs. Buchanan's car on horses and Phoebe was intent on pinning up the débutante's habit skirt to a comfortable scramble length. Billy Bob fairly bubbled over with glee and Milly, who had come to assist Mrs. Matilda in overlooking the preparations for the feast for the returned hunters, was already busy assembling hampers and cases on a flat rock over behind the largest fire. Her anxious heart was at rest about her nestlings, for Caroline's maid, Annette, had gone French mad over the babies and had begged the privilege of keeping Mammy Betty company in her watch beside the cots.

"Come here, Caroline, child," called David from behind the farthest fire, "let me look at you! Seems to me you are in for a good freezing." And he drew her into the light of the blaze.

She was kilted and booted and coated and belted in the most beautiful and wholly correct attire for the hunt that could possibly have been contrived; that is, for a sedate cross-country bird stalk or a decorous trap shooting, but for a long night scramble over the frozen ground she was insufficiently clad. The other girls all wore heavy golf skirts and coats and were muffled to their eyes; even the big-bug lady wore a knitted comforter high round her throat. Without doubt Caroline would have been in for a cold deal, if David had not been more than equal to any occasion.

"Here, Andy, skin out of that sweater and get into that extra buckskin in my electric," he said, and forthwith began without ceremony to assist Andrew Sevier in peeling off a soft, white, high-collared sweater he wore, and in less time than it took to think it he had slipped it over Caroline's protesting head, pulled it down around her slim hips almost to where her kilts met her boots and rolled the collar up under her eyes. Then he immediately turned his attention to the arrival of the mongrel sleuths, each accompanied by a white-toothed negro of renowned coon-fighting, possum-catching proclivities, whom he had assembled from the Old Harpeth to lead the hunt, thus leaving Caroline and Andrew alone for the moment on the far side of the fire.

"Indeed, I'm not going to have your sweater!" she protested, beginning to divest herself of the borrowed garment, but not knowing exactly how to crawl out of its soft embrace.

"Please, oh, please do!" he exclaimed quickly, and as he spoke he caught her hand away, that had begun to tug at the collar.

"I wouldn't keep it for the world—and have you cold, but—I can't get out," she answered with a laugh. "Please show me or call for help."

And as she pleaded Andrew Sevier towered beside her, tall and slender, while the cold breeze with its pine-laden breath ruffled his white shirt-sleeves across his arms. Caroline Darrah in the embrace of his clinging apparel was a sight that sent the blood through his veins at a rate that warred with the winds, and his eyes drank deeply. The color mounted under her eyes and with the unconsciousness of a child she nestled her chin in the woolly folds about the neck as she turned her face from the firelight.

"Well, then, get David's coat from the car," she pleaded.

"Will you stand back in the shadow of that tree until I do?" he asked.

He had caught across the fire a glimpse of the restive Hobson and a sudden mad desire prompted him to snatch this one joy from Fate, come what would—just a few hours with her under the winter stars, when life seemed to offer so little in the count of the years.

"Why, yes, of course! Did you think I'd dare go out in the dark alone, without you?" and her joyous ingenuous casting of herself upon his protection was positively poignant. "Hurry, please, because I—don't want anybody to find me before you come!" After which request it took him very little time to run across the lot and vault the fence into the road where the electric stood.

"It's so uncertain how things arrange themselves sometimes, some places," she remarked to herself as she caught sight of the movements of the foiled Hobson, whose search had now become an open maneuver.

Suddenly she laid her cheek against the arm of the sweater and sniffed it with her delicate nose—yes, there was the undeniable fragrance of the major's Seven Oaks heart-leaf. "He steals the tobacco, too," she again remarked to herself as she caught sight of him skirting the fires as he returned.

Just at this moment a pandemonium of yelps, barks, bays and yells broke forth up the ravine and declared the hunt on.

"Everybody follow the dogs and keep within hearing distance! We'll wait for the trailers to come up when we tree before we shake down!" shouted David as with one accord the whole company plunged into the woods.

Away from the fire, the starlight, which was beginning to be reinforced by the glow from a late old moon, was bright enough to keep the rush up the ravine, over log and boulder, through tangle and across open, a not too dangerous foray.

The first hurdle was a six-rail fence that snaked its way between a frozen meadow and a woods lot. David stationed himself on the far side of the lowest and strongest panel and proceeded to swing down the girls whom Hob and Tom persuaded to the top rail.

The champion for the rights of women took long and much

assistance for the mount and entrusted her somewhat bulky self to the strong arms of David Kildare with a feminine dependence that almost succeeded in cracking those stalwart supports.

Polly climbed two rails, put her hand on the top and vaulted like a boy almost into the embrace of young Massachusetts and together they raced after the dogs, who were adding tumult to the hitherto pandemonium of the hot trail.

Tom Cantrell managed Mrs. Cherry most deftly and seemed anxious to direct David in the landing though she was most willing to trust it entirely to him. After hurrying Phoebe to the top rail he vaulted lightly to the side of David and departed in haste, taking the reluctant widow with him by main force.

Phoebe perched herself on the top of the fence, which brought her head somewhat above the level of David's, and seemed in no hurry to descend in order to be at the shake-down, which from the shouts and yelps seemed imminent.

"Ready, or want to rest a minute?" asked David gently; but his eyes looked past hers and there was the shadow of reserve in his voice.

"No," answered Phoebe, "but you must be tired so I'll just slip down," and she essayed to cheat him with the utmost treachery. David neither spoke nor looked at her directly but took her quietly in his arms and swung her to the ground beside him.

Now this was not the first pursuit of the possum that had been attended by Phoebe in the company of David Kildare, and she was prepared for the audacious hint of a squeeze, with which he usually took his toll and which she always ignored utterly with reproving intent; the more reproving on the one or two occasions when she had been tempted into yielding to the caress for the remotest fraction of a second. But for every snub in the fence events that had been pulled off between them in the past years, David was fully revenged by the impassive landing of Phoebe on the dry and frozen grass at his side. Revenged—and there was something over that was cutting into her adamant heart like a two-edge marble saw.

But Phoebe had been born a thoroughbred and it was head up and run as she saw in a second, so she smiled up at him and said in a perfectly friendly tone:

"I really don't think we'd better wait for Caroline and Andrew. Do let's hurry, for they've treed, and I think those dogs will go mad in a moment!" And together they disappeared in the woodland.

Around a tall tree that stood on the slope of the hill they found a scene that was uproar rampant. Five maddened dogs gazed aloft into the gnarled branches of the persimmon king and danced and jumped to the accompaniment of one another's insane yelps. A half-dozen negro boys were in the same attitude and state of mind, and the tension was immense.

Polly gasped and giggled and the suffrage lady almost became entangled with the waltzing dogs in her endeavor to sight the quarry.

"Dar he am!" exclaimed the blackest satyr, and he pointed to one of the lower limbs from which there hung by the tail the most pathetic little bunch of bristles imaginable. "Le'me shake him down, Mister David, I foun' him!"

"All right, shin up, but mind the limbs," answered David. "And you, Jake, get the dogs in hand! We want to take home possums, not full dogs!"

And like an agile ape the darky swung himself up and out on the low limb. "Here he come!" he shouted, and ducked to give a jerk that shook the whole limb.

The dogs danced and Polly squealed, while the rotund lady

managed to step on young Back Bay's toes and almost forgot to "beg pardon," but Mr. Possum hung on by his long rat-tail with the greatest serenity.

"Buck up thar, nigger, shake dat whole tree; dis here ain't no cake-walk," one of his confrères yelled, and the sally was caught with a loud guffaw.

Thus urged the darky braced himself and succeeded in putting the whole tree into a commotion, at the height of which there was a crash and a scramble from the top limb and in a second a ball of gray fur descended on his woolly head, knocked him off his perch and crashed with him to the ground. Then there ensued a raging battle in which were involved five dogs, a long darky and a ring-tailed streak of coon lightning, which whirled and bit and scratched itself free and plunged into the darkness before the astonished hunters could get more than a glimpse of the mêlée.

"Coon, coon!" yelled the negroes, and scattered into the woods at the heels of the discountenanced dogs. Mr. Possum, saved by the stiff fight put up by his ring-tailed woods-brother, had taken this opportunity of unhanging himself and departing into parts unknown, perhaps a still more wily citizen after his threatened extinction.

In a few minutes from up the hill came another tumult, and Jake raised a long shout of "two possums," which served to hasten the scramble of the rest of the party through the underbrush to a breathless pace.

Another gray ball hung to another limb and this time the derisive Jake succeeded in the shake-down and the bagging amid the most breathless excitement. It was a sight to see the sophisticated little animal lie like dead and be picked up and handled in a state of seeming lifeless rigidity—a display of self-control that seemed to argue a superiority of instinct over reason.

After this opening event the hunt swept on with a rapidly mounting count and a heavier and heavier bag.

And, too, it was just as well that no one in particular, save the defrauded Hobson, who was obliged to conceal his chagrin, was especially mindful of the whereabouts of Caroline and the poet. In fact, it would have been difficult for them to have located themselves in answer to a wireless inquiry.

Andrew had started out from the hiding tree with the intention of cutting across the trail of the hunters at right angles a little up the ravine, and he had trusted to a six-year-old remembrance of the lay of the land as he led the way across the frosty meadow and up the ridge at a brisk pace. Caroline swung lithely along beside him and in the matter of fences took Polly's policy of a hand up and then a high vault, which made for practically no delay. They skirted the tangle of buck bushes and came out on the edge of the cliff just as the hunt swept by at their feet and on up the creek bed. They were both breathless and tingling with the exertion of their climb.

"There they go—left behind—no catching them!" exclaimed Andrew. "No possum for you, and this is your hunt! I'm most awfully sorry!"

"Don't you suppose they will save me one?" asked Caroline composedly, and as she spoke she walked to the edge of the bluff and looked down into the dark ravine interestedly.

"You don't want the possum, child, you want to see it caught. The negroes get the little beasts; it's the bagging that's the excitement!" Andrew regarded her with amused interest.

"I don't seem to care to see things caught," she answered. "I'm always sorry for them. I would let them all go if I got the chance—all caught things." A little crackle in the bushes at her side made her move nearer to him.

"I believe you would—release any 'caught thing'—if you

could," he said with a note of bitterness in his voice that she failed to detect. A cold wind swept across the meadow and he swung around so his broad shoulders screened her from its tingle. Her eyes gazed out over the valley at their feet.

"This is the edge of the world," she said softly. "Do you remember your little verses about the death of the stars?" She turned and raised her eyes to his. "We are holding a death-watch beside them now as the moon comes up over the ridge there. When I read the poem I felt breathless to get out somewhere high up and away from things—and watch."

"I was 'high up' when I wrote them," answered Andrew with a laugh. "Look over there on the hill—see those two old locusts? They are fern palms and those scrub oaks are palmettos. The white frost makes the meadow a lagoon and this rock is the pier of my bridge where I came out to watch one night to test the force of a freshet. Over there the light from Mrs. Matilda's fires is the construction camp and beyond that hill is my bungalow. That's the same old moon that's rising relentlessly to murder the stars again. Do you want to stay and watch the tragedy—or hunt?"

Without a word Caroline sank down on the dried leaves that lay in a drift on the edge of the bluff. Andrew crouched close beside her to the windward. And the ruthless old moon that was putting the stars out of business by the second was not in the least abashed to find them gazing at her as she blustered up over the ridge, round and red with exertion.

"Were you alone on that pier?" asked Caroline with the utmost naïveté, as she snuggled down deeper into the collar of the sweater.

"I'm generally alone—in most ways," answered Andrew, the suspicion of a laugh covering the sadness in his tone. "I seem to see myself going through life alone unless something happens—quick!" The bitter note sounded plainly this time and cut with an ache into her consciousness.

"I've been a little lonely, too—always, until just lately and now I don't feel that way at all;" she looked at him thoughtfully with moonlit eyes that were deep like sapphires. "I wonder why?"

Andrew Sevier's heart stopped dead still for a second and then began to pound in his breast as if entrapped. For the moment his voice was utterly useless and he prayed helplessly for a meed of self-control that might aid him to gain a sane footing.

Then just at that moment the old genie of the forests, who gloats through the seasons over myriads of wooings that are carried on in the fastnesses of his green woods, sounded a long, low, guttural groan that rose to a blood-curdling shriek, from the branches just above the head of the moon-mad man and girl. For an instrument he used the throat of an enraged old hoot-owl, perturbed by the intrusion of the noise of the distant hunt and the low-voiced conversation on his wonted privacy.

And the experienced ancient succeeded in precipitating the crisis of the situation with magical promptness, for Caroline sprang to her feet, turned with a shudder and buried her head in Andrew's hunting coat somewhere near the left string for cartridge loops. She clung to him in abject terror.

"Sweetheart!" he exclaimed, giving her a little shake, "it's only a cross old owl—don't be frightened," and he raised her cheek against his own and drew her nearer. But Caroline trembled and clung and seemed unable to face the situation. Andrew essayed further reassurance by turning his head until his lips pressed a tentative kiss against the curve of her chin.

"He can't get you," he entreated and managed a still closer embrace.

"Is he still there?" came in a muffled voice from against his neck where Caroline had again buried her head at a slight crackling from the dark branches overhead.

"I think he is, bless him!" answered Andrew, and this time the kiss managed a landing on the warm lips under the eyes raised to his.

And then ensued several breathless moments while the world reeled around and the vital elemental force that is sometimes cruel, sometimes kind, turned the wheel of their universe.

"I'm not frightened any more," Caroline at last managed to say as she prepared to withdraw, not too decisively, from her strong-armed refuge.

"He's still there," warned Andrew Sevier with a happy laugh, and Caroline yielded again for a second, then drew his arms aside.

"Thank you—I'm not afraid any more—of anything," she said, laughing into his eyes, "and I really think we had better try to get back to camp and supper, for I don't hear the dogs any longer. We don't want to be lost like the 'babes in the woods' and left to die out here, do we?"

"Are you sure we haven't gone and stumbled into heaven, anyway?" demanded Andrew.

He then proceeded to roll the collar of her sweater higher about her ears and to pull the long sleeves down over her hands. He even bent to stretch the garment an inch or two nearer the tops of her boots.

"Are you cold?" he demanded anxiously, for a stiff wind had risen and blew upon them with icy breath.

"Not a single bit," she answered, submitting herself to his anxious ministrations with her most engaging six-going-on-seven manner. Then she caught one of his fumbling hands in hers and pressed it to her cheek for a moment.

"Now," she said, "we can never be lonely any more, can we?

I'm going to race you down the hill, across the meadow and over three fences to supper!" And before he could stay her she had flitted through the bushes and was running on before him, slim and fleet.

He caught her in time to swing her over the first fence and capture an elusive caress. The second barrier she vaulted and eluded him entirely, but from the top of the last she bent and gave him his kiss as he lifted her down. In another moment they had joined the circle around the crackling fire, where they were greeted with the wildest hilarity and overwhelmed with food and banter.

"Did you people ever hear of the man who bought a fifty-dollar coon dog, took him out to hunt the first night, almost cried because he thought he had lost him down a sink hole, hunted all night for him, came home in the daylight and found pup asleep under the kitchen stove?" demanded David as he filled two long glasses with a simmering decoction, from which arose the aroma of baked apples, spices, and some of the major's eighty-six corn heart. "Caroline is my point to my little story. Have you two been sitting in Mrs. Matilda's car or mine, or did you roost for a time on the fence over there in the dark?"

"Please, David, please hush and give me a bird and a biscuit— I'm hungry," answered Caroline as she sank on a cushion beside Mrs. Buchanan.

"According to the ink slingers of all times you ought not to be; but Andy has already got outside of two sandwiches, so I suppose you are due one small bird. That cake is grand, beautiful. I've put it away to eat all by myself to-morrow. Andrew Sevier doesn't need any. He wouldn't know cake from corn-pone—he's moonstruck."

Just at this point a well-aimed pine-cone glanced off David's collar and he settled down to the business in hand, which was the disposal of a bursting and perfectly hot potato, handed fresh from the coals by the attentive Jeff.

And it was more than an hour later that the tired hunters wended their way back to the city. Polly was so sleepy that she could hardly sit her horse and was in a subdued and utterly fascinating mood, with which she did an irreparable amount of damage to the stranger within her gates as she rode along the moonlit pike, and for which she had later to make answer. The woman's champion dozed in the tonneau and only David had the spirit to sing as they whirled along.

Hadn't Phoebe stirred the sugar into his cup of coffee and then in an absolutely absent-minded manner tasted it before she had come around the fire to hand it to him? It had been a standing argument between them for years as to a man's right to this small attention, which they both teased Mrs. Matilda for bestowing upon the major. It was an insignificant, inconsequent little ceremony in itself but it fired a train in David's mind, made for healing the wound in his heart and brought its consequences. Another reconstruction campaign began to shape its policy in the mind of David Kildare which had to do with the molding of the destiny of the high-headed young woman of his affections, rather than with the amelioration of conditions in his native city. So, high and clear he sang the call of the mocking-bird with its ecstasies and its minors.

But late as it was, after he had landed his guests at their doors, he had a long talk over the phone with the clerk of his headquarters and sent a half-dozen telegrams before he turned into his room. When he switched on his lights he saw that Andrew stood by the window looking out into the night. His face was so drawn and white as he turned that David started and reached out to lay a hand on his shoulder.

"Dave," he said, "I'm a blackguard and a coward—don't touch me!"

"What is it, Andrew?" asked David as he laid his arm across the tense shoulders.

"I thought I was strong and dared to stay—now I know I'm a coward and couldn't go. I'll have to sneak away and leave her—hurt!" His voice was low and toned with an unspeakable scorn of himself.

"Andy," asked David, as he swung him around to face him, "was Caroline Darrah too much for you—and the moon?"

"There's nothing to say about it, David, nothing! I have only made it hard for her: and killed myself for myself forever. She's a child and she'll forget. You'll see to her, won't you?"

"What are you going to do now?" asked David sternly.

"Cut and run—cowards always do," answered Andrew bitterly. "I am going to stay and see you through this election, for it's too late to turn the press matters over to any one else—and I'm going to pray to find some way to make it easier for her before I leave her. I'm afraid some day she'll find out—and not understand why I went."

"Why do you go, Andrew?" asked David as he faced this friend with compelling eyes. "If it's pride that takes you, better give it up! It's deadly for you both, for she's more of a woman than you think—she'll suffer."

"David, do you think she would have me if she knew what I put aside to take her—*and his millions*? Could Peters Brown's heiress ever have anything but contempt for me? When it comes to her she must understand—and not think I held it against her!"

"Tell her, Andrew; let her decide! It's her right now!"

"Never," answered Andrew passionately. "She is just beginning to lose some of her sensitiveness among us and this is the worst of all the things she has felt were between her and her people.

It is the only thing he covered and hid from her. I'll *never* tell her—I'll go—and she will forget!" In his voice there was the note of finality that is unmistakable from man to man. He turned toward his room as he finished speaking.

"Then, boy," said David as he held him back for a second in the bend of his arm, a tenderness in voice and clasp, "go if you must; but we've three days yet. The gods can get mighty busy in that many hours if they pull on a woman's side—which they always do. Good night!"

CHAPTER X

LOVE'S HOME AND ANDREW SEVIER

And the Sabbath quiet which had descended on the frost-jeweled city the morning after the hunt found the Buchanan household still deep in close-shuttered sleep. Their fatigue demanded and was having its way in the processes of recuperation and they all slept on serenely.

Only Caroline Darrah was astir with the first deep notes of the early morning bells. Her awaking had come with a rush of pure, bubbling, unalloyed joy which turned her cheeks the hue of the rose, starred her eyes and melted her lips into heavenly curves. In her exquisite innocence it never dawned upon her that the moments spent in Andrew's arms under the winter moon were any but those of rapturous betrothal and her love had flowered in confident happiness. It was well that she caught across the distance no hint of the battle that was being waged in the heart of Andrew Sevier, for the man in him fought (for her) with what he deemed his honor, almost to the death—but not quite, for some men hold as honor that which is strong sinewed with self-control, red blooded with courage, infiltrated with pride and ruthlessly cruel.

And so Caroline hummed David's little serenade to herself as she dressed without Annette's assistance and smiled at her own radiance reflected at her from her mirrors. She had just completed a most ravishing church toilet when she heard the major's door close softly and she knew that now she would find him before his logs awaiting breakfast.

She blushed another tone more rosy and her eyes grew shy at the very thought of meeting his keen eyes that always quizzed her with such delight after one of her initiations into the sports or gaieties of this new country. But assuming her courage with her prayer-book, she softly descended the stairs, crossed the hall and stood beside his chair with a laugh of greeting.

"Well," he demanded delightedly though in a guarded tone with a glance up as if at Mrs. Matilda's and Phoebe's closed doors, "did you catch your possum?"

"Yes—that is—no! I didn't, but somebody did I think," she answered with delicious confusion in both tone and appearance.

"Caroline Darrah," demanded the major, "do you mean to tell me that there is no certainty of anybody's having got a result from a foray of the magnitude of that last night? Didn't you even see a possum?"

"No, I didn't; but I know they caught some—David said so," answered Caroline in a reassuring voice.

"Caroline," again demanded the major relentlessly, having already had his suspicions aroused by her confusion and blushes, "where were you when David Kildare caught those beasts that you didn't see one?"

"I was—was lost," she answered, and it surprised him that she didn't put one rosy finger-tip into her mouth, so very young was her further confusion.

"Alone?" The major made his demand without mercy.

"No, sir, with Mr. Sevier—why, aren't you going to have breakfast, Major, it is almost church time?" and Caroline rallied her domestic dignity to her support as she escaped toward Temple's domain.

And the flush of joy that had flamed in her cheeks had lighted a glow in the major's weather-tanned old face and his eyes fairly snapped with light. Could it be that the boy had reached out for his atonement? Could it be—he heard the front door close as the first church bell struck a deep note and at that moment Jeff announced his breakfast as ready in a voice of the deepest exhaustion.

And when Caroline emerged from the still darkened house into the crisp air she found Andrew Sevier standing on the front steps waiting to walk into church with her.

Her smile of shy joy as she held out her hand to him warmed his somber eyes for the moment.

"They are all asleep," she whispered as if even from the street there was danger of awakening the tired hunting party. "The major is keeping it quiet for them."

"And you ought to be asleep, too," he answered as they started off at a brisk pace down the avenue.

"*You* weren't," she laughed up at him, and then dropped her eyes shyly. "I always go to church," she added demurely.

"And I suppose I counted on your habit," he said, utterly unable to control the tenderness in voice or glance.

"I wanted you to go with me to-day—I hoped you would though you never have," she answered him with a divine seriousness in her lifted eyes. "They are all coming to dinner and then you'll go to the office, so I hoped about this morning." She was utterly lovely in her gentleness and a strange peace fell into the troubled heart of the man at her side.

And it followed him into the dim church and made the hour

he sat at her side one of holy healing. Once as they knelt together during the service she slipped her gloved hand into his for an instant and from its warmth there flowed a strength of which he stood in dire need and from which he drew courage to go on for the few days remaining before his exile. Just to protect her, he prayed, and leave her unhurt, and he failed to see that the humility and blindness of a great love were leading him into the perpetration of a great cruelty, to the undoing of them both.

Then in the long days that followed so hunted was he by his love of her that that one hour of peace in the Sunday morning was all he dared give himself with her. And in her gentle trustfulness it was not hard to make his excuses, for the Monday morning brought the strenuosity in the career of David Kildare to a state of absolute acuteness.

To the candidate the three days were as ten years crowded into as many hours. Down at his headquarters in the *Gray Picket* rooms he stood firm and met wave after wave of fluctuating excitement that surged around him with his head up, a ring in his laugh and an almost superhuman tact.

As late as Wednesday noon there appeared before him three excited Anti-Saloon League matrons with plans to put committees of ladies at all the polls to hand out lemonade and entreaties—perhaps threats—to the voters as they exercised their civic function. They had planned banners with "Shall The Saloon Have My Boy?" in large letters thereon inscribed and they were morally certain that without the carrying out of their plan the day would be lost. It took David Kildare one hour and a quarter to persuade them that it would be better to have a temperance rally at the theater on Wednesday night at which each of the three should make most convincing speeches to the assembled women of the city, thereby furnishing arguments to their sisters with which to start the men to the polls next day.

He promised to come and make a short opening speech and

they left him with their plans changed but their enthusiasm augmented. David sank into a chair and mopped his shining brow. The major had been witness to the encounter from the editorial desk and Cap Cantrell was bent double with laughter behind a pile of papers he was searching for data for Andrew.

"I'm all in, Major," said David faintly. "Just pick up the pieces in a basket."

"David, sir," said the major, "your conduct of that onslaught was masterly! If the hand that rocks the cradle rules the world why not the hand that flips the batter-cake rock the ballot-box—cradle out of date? That's a little mixed but pertinent. I'm for letting them have the try. They're only crying because they think we don't want 'em to have it—maybe they'll go back to the cradle and rock all the better for being free citizens!"

"And not a cussed one of those three old lady cats has ever shown a kitten!" exploded Cap from behind his pile of papers.

"Anyway, the worst is over now—must be!" answered David as he began to read over some bulletins and telegrams. But he had troubles yet to come. In the next two hours he had a conference with the head of the chamber of commerce which heated his blood to the boiling-point and brought forth an ultimatum, delivered in no uncertain terms but with such perfect courtesy and clean-sightedness that the gentleman departed in haste to look into certain matters which he now suspected to have been cooked to lead him astray.

This event had been followed by the advent of five of the old fellows who had obtained furloughs and ridden in from the Soldiers' Home for the express purpose of assuring him of their support, as the vindicator of their honor, wringing his hand and cheering on the fight. They retired with Cap into the back room and emerged shortly, beaming and refreshed. They had no votes to cast in the city, but what matter?

On their heels, Mike O'Rourke rushed in with two budgets of false registrations which he had been able to ferret out by the aid of the drivers of his grocery wagons. He embraced David, exchanged shots with the major, and departed in high spirits. Then quiet came to the *Gray Picket* for a time and Kildare plunged into his papers with desperation.

"David," called the major after a very few minutes of peace, "here's a call for you on the desk. You'll recognize the number—remember, a firm hand, sir—a firm hand!" with which he collected his hat, coat, and the captain and took his departure, leaving David for the moment alone in the editorial rooms.

He sat for a few moments before the receiver and twisted the call slip around one of his fingers. In a moment the affairs of state and the destiny of the city slipped from his shoulders and his mind took up the details of another problem.

The contest for the judgeship was not the only one David Kildare had taken upon himself—the second was being waged in the secret chambers of two hearts, one proud, exacting and unconvinced, the other determined and at last thoroughly aroused. Phoebe had brought the crisis on herself and she was beginning to realize that the duel would be to the death or complete surrender.

And in the preliminaries, which had been begun on the Saturday night hunt and carried on for the last three days, David Kildare had failed to make a single false move. His natural and inevitable absorption in his race for the judgeship had served to keep him from forcing a single issue; and Phoebe had had time to do a little lonely, unpursued thinking.

He had been entirely too clever to arouse her pride against him by a suspicion of neglect in his attitude. His usual attentions were all offered and a new one or two contrived. He sent Eph to report to her with his electric every afternoon—she understood that he was unable by the exigencies of the case to come himself to take her to keep her appointments as was his custom. Her flowers were just as thoughtfully selected and sent with the gayest little notes, as like as possible to the ones that had been coming to her for years. He ordered in an unusually large basket of eggs from the farm and managed to find a complicated arrangement of rope and pulleys, the manipulation of which for an hour or more daily was warranted to add to or detract from the stature of man or woman, according to the desire of the dissatisfied individual. His note with the instrument was a scintillating skit and was answered in kind. But through it all Phoebe was undoubtedly lonely. This call, the second since Saturday and the second in the history of their joint existences, betrayed her to the now wily David more than she realized—perhaps!

He took down the receiver and got the connection.

"That you—dear?" David managed a casual voice with difficulty.

"Yes, David," came in a voice that fairly radiated across the city. "I only wanted to ask how it goes."

"Fine—with a rip! But you never can tell—about anything. I'm a Presbyterian and I'll die in doubt of my election. I'm learning not to count on—things." His voice carried a mournful note that utterly belied his radiant face. David was enjoying himself to almost the mortal limit!

"David," there was a perceptible pause—"you—there is one thing you can always count on—isn't there—*me*?" The voice was very gallant but also slightly palpitating. David almost lost his head but hung on tight and came up right side.

"Some," he answered, which reply, in the light of an extremely modern use of the word combined with the legitimate, was calculated to bring conclusion. Then he hurried another offering on to the wire.

"How long are you going to be at home?" he asked—another dastardly tantalization.

"I—I don't know exactly," she parried quickly. "Why?" and this from Phoebe who had always granted interviews like a queen gives jewels! David somewhere found the courage to lay a firm hand on himself. With just a few more blows the citadel was his! His own heart writhed and the uncertainty made him quake internally.

"I wish I could come over, but there are two committees waiting in the other room for me. Do you—" a clash and buzz hummed over the wire into the receiver. There was a jangle and tangle and a rough man's voice cut in with, "Working on the wires, hang up, please," and David limply hung up the receiver and collapsed in solitude, for his committees had been evoked out of thin air.

His state of mind was positively abject. His years-old tenderness welled up in his heart and flooded to his eyes—the dash and the pluck of her! He reached for his hat, then hesitated; it was election eve and in two hours he was due to address the congregation of griddle-cake discontents on how to make men vote like ladies.

A call boy hurried in by way of a fortunate distraction and handed in a budget of papers. David spread them out before him. They were from Susie Carrie of the strong brush and the Civic Improvement League, containing Sketches and specifications for the drinking fountains already pledged, and a request for an early institution of legislation on the play-ground proposition. Such a small thing as an uncertain election failed to daunt the artistic fervor of Susie Carrie's fertile brain or to deter her from making demands, however premature, on David the sympathetic.

And David Kildare dropped his head on the papers and groaned. The Vision of a life-work rose up and menaced him and the words "sweat of his brow" for the first time took on a concrete meaning. Such a good, old, care-free existence he was losing, and—he seized his hat and fled to the refreshment of bath, food and fresh raiment.

And on his way home he stopped in for a word with the major, whom he found tired and on his way to take as much as he could of his usual nap. He was seated in his chair by the table and Caroline Darrah sat near him, listening eagerly to his story of some of the events in the day's campaign. She rose as David entered and held out her hand to him with a smile.

Every time David had looked at Caroline Darrah for the few days past a sharp pain had cut into his heart and this afternoon she was so radiantly lovely with sympathy and interest that for a moment he stood looking at her with his eyes full of tenderness. Then he managed a bantering smile and backed away a step or two from her, his hands behind him.

"No, you don't, beautiful," David sometimes ventured on Phoebe's name for the girl, "you are so sweet in that frock that I'm afraid if I touch you I'll stick. Somebody ought to label such a lollypop as you dangerous. Call her off, Major!"

The major laughed at Caroline's blush and laid his fingers over her hand that rested on the corner of the table near him.

"David," he said, "girls are confections to which it is good for a man to forsake all others and cling—but not to gobble. Matilda, recount to David Kildare your plans for the night of the election. I wish to witness his joy."

"Oh, yes, I've been wanting to tell you about it for two days, David, dear," answered Mrs. Buchanan from her chair over by the window where she was busily engaged in checking names off a long list with a pencil. "We are going to have a reception at the University Club so everybody can come and congratulate you the night of the election. Mrs. Shelby and I thought it up and of course we had to speak to one of the house committee about the arrangements, and who do you think the member was—Billy Bob! I just talked on and didn't notice Mrs. Shelby and finally he was so nice and deferential to her that she talked some, too. She almost started to shake hands with him when we left. I was so glad. I feel that it is going to be a delightful success in every way. Please be thinking up a nice speech to make."

"Oh, wait," groaned David Kildare, "if I begin now I will have to think double, one for election and one for defeat. Last night I dreamed about a black cat that was minus a left eye and limped in the right hind leg. Jeff almost cried when I told him about it. He hasn't smiled since."

"I told Tempie to put less pepper in those chicken croquettes last night—I saw Phoebe's light burning until two o'clock and heard her and Caroline laughing and talking even after that. The major was so nervous that he was up and dressed at six o'clock. I must see that all of you get simpler food—your nerves will suffer. Major, suppose you don't eat much dinner—just have a little milk toast. I'll see Tempie about it now!" and Mrs. Buchanan departed after bestowing a glance, in which was a conviction of dyspepsia, upon all three of them.

"Now, David Kildare, see what you've done with your black-cat crawlings! I'll have to eat that toast—see if I don't! I've consumed it with a smile during stated periods for thirty years. Yes, girl-love is a kind of cup-custard, but wife-love is bread and butter—milk toast, for instance—bless her! But I am hungry!" The major's expression was a tragedy.

"I'm going to try and beg you off, Major, dear," said Caroline Darrah, and she hurried after Mrs. Matilda into Tempie's domain.

"Major," said David as he gazed after the girl, "when I look at her I feel cold all over, then hot-mad! He's going to-morrow night on the midnight train—and she doesn't know! I can't even talk to him about it—he looks like a dead man and works like a demon. I don't know what to do!"

"David," said the major slowly as he pressed the tips of his long lean fingers together and regarded them intently, "how love, tender wise love, love that is fed on heart's blood and lives by soul-breath, can go deaf, blind, dumb, halt, broken-winged, idiotic and mortally cruel is more than I can see. God Almighty comfort him when he finds what he has done!"

"And if she does find it out she won't understand," exclaimed David.

"No," answered the major, "she doesn't even suspect anything. She thinks it is the press of his work that keeps him away from her. The child carries about with her that aura of transport that only an acknowledgment from a lover can give a woman. I had hoped that he had seen some way—I couldn't ask! I wonder—"

"Yes, Major," interrupted David quickly, and he winced as he spoke, "it happened on the hunt Saturday evening. They climbed the bluff and watched the hunt from a distance and I saw how it was the minute they came back to the campfire. I saw it and I was just jolly happy over it even to the tune of Phoebe's sulks—I thought it was all right, and I wish you could have seen him. His head was up and his eyes danced and he gave up almost the first real laugh I ever heard from him, when I teased her about getting lost. As I looked at him I thought about the other, your glad Andrew, Major, and I was happy all in a shot for you, because I thought you were going to get back something of what you'd lost. It all seemed so good!"

"There's been joy in the boy's eyes, joy and sorrow waging a war for weeks, David, and I've had to sit by and watch, powerless to help him. Yes, his very father himself has looked out of his eyes at me for moments and I—well I had hoped. Are you sure he is going?" As the major asked the question his brows knotted themselves together as if to hide the pain in his eyes.

"Yes, he's going and he catches the next tramp steamer for Panama from Savannah. I wish she would suspect something and force it from him. It's strange she doesn't," answered David despondently.

"Caroline Darrah belongs to the order of humble women whose love feeds on a glance and can be sustained on a crumb—another class demands a banquet full spread and always ready. You'll be careful, boy, don't—don't diet Phoebe too long!" The major eyed David anxiously across the light.

"Heavens, I'm your reconcentrado! Major, I feel as if I'd been shut up down cellar in the cold without the breath of life for a year. It's only three days and thirteen hours and a half; but I'm all in. I go dead without her—believe I'll telephone her now!" And David reached for the receiver that stood on the major's table.

"Now, David," said the major, restraining his eager hand and smiling through his sadness, "don't try to gather your grapes over the phone! I judge they are ripe, but they still hang high—they always will! Look at the clock!"

David took one look at the staid old mahogany timepiece, which the major had had brought in from Seven Oaks and placed in the corner opposite his table, and took his departure.

And after he had gone the major retired to his room to lie down for as much of his allotted rest as he could obtain. Seeing him safely settled, Mrs. Buchanan went over for a short visit with Mrs. Shelby next door. Mrs. Matilda stuck to the irate grandmother through thick and thin and in her affectionate heart she had hopes of bringing about the much to be desired reconciliation. She was the only person in the city who dared mention Milly or the babies to the old lady and even in her unsophistication she suspected that the details she supplied with determined intrepidity fed a hunger in the lonely old heart. Her pilgrimage next door was a daily one and never neglected.

Thus left alone Caroline Darrah was partaking of a solitary cup of tea, which was being served her by Tempie in all the gorgeousness of a new white lace-trimmed and beruffled apron which Caroline had made for her as near as possible like the dainty garments affected by the French shop-clad Annette, who was Temple's special ally and admirer, when Mrs. Cherry Lawrence, in full regalia, descended upon her. Tempie walled her black eyes and departed with dignity for an extra cup.

The major was fast asleep, David Kildare in the processes of bath and toilet, Phoebe at her desk down-town and Mrs. Matilda away on her mission, and thus it happened that nobody was near to fend the blight from the flower of their anxious cherishing.

"Yes, indeed, it is a time of anxiety," Mrs. Cherry agreed with Caroline as she crushed the lemon in her tea. "I shall be glad when it is over. I feel that we all are making the utmost sacrifices for this election of David Kildare's, and he's such a boy that he probably will make a perfectly impossible judge. He never takes anything seriously enough to accomplish much. It's well for him that no one expects anything from him."

"Oh, but I'm sure he's taking this seriously," exclaimed Caroline Darrah with a little gleam of dismay in her eyes. "His race has been an exceptional one whether he wins or not. The major says so and the other day Mr. Sevier told me—" At the mention of Andrew Sevier's name Mrs. Cherry glanced around and an ugly little gleam came into her eyes.

"Oh, of course Andrew Sevier is too loyal to admit any criticism of David to a *stranger*," she said with a slight emphasis on the word and a cold glance at Caroline Darrah.

"But he wasn't talking to a stranger, he was talking just to me," said Caroline quickly, not even seeing the dart aimed.

"You are so sweet, dear!" purred Mrs. Cherry. "Under the circumstances it is so gracious of you not to feel yourself a stranger with us all and especially with Andrew Sevier. Of course it would have been impossible for him always to have avoided you and it was just like his generosity—"

"Miss Ca'line, honey," came in a decided voice from the doorway, "that custard you is a-making for the major's supper is actin' curisome around the aiges. Please, ma'am, come and see ter it a minute!"

"Oh, excuse me just a second," exclaimed Caroline Darrah to Mrs. Cherry as she rose with alarm in her housewifely heart and hurried past Tempie down the hall.

An instinct engendered by her love for Caroline Darrah had led Tempie to notice and resent something in Mrs. Lawrence's manner to the child on several previous occasions and to-day she had felt no scruples about remaining behind the curtains well within ear-shot of the conversations. Her knowledge of, and participation in, the Buchanan family affairs, past and present and future, was an inheritance of several generations and she never hesitated to assert her privileges.

"Lady," she said in a cool soft voice as she squared herself in the doorway and looked Mrs. Lawrence directly in the face, "you is a rich white woman and I's a poor nigger, but ef you had er secceeded in a-putting that thare devil's tale into my young mistess's head they would er been that 'twixt you and me that we never would er forgot; and there wouldn't a-been more'n a rag left of that dead-husband-bought frock what you've got on. Now 'fore I fergits myself I axes you out the front door—and I'm a-fergittin' fast."

And as she faced the domineering woman in her trappings of fashion all the humble blood in the negro's veins, which had come down to her from the forewomen who had cradled on their black breasts the mothers of such as Caroline Darrah, was turned into the jungle passion for defense of this slight white thing that was the child of her heart if not of her body. The danger of it made Mrs. Lawrence fairly quail, and, white with fright, she gathered her rich furs about her and fled just as Caroline Darrah's returning footsteps were heard in the hall.

"Why, where did Mrs. Lawrence go, Tempie?" she demanded in astonishment. Tempie had just the moment in which to rally herself but she had accomplished the feat, though her eyes still rolled ominously.

"She 'membered something what she forgot and had ter hurry. She lef' scuses fer you," and Tempie busied herself with the cups and tray.

"She was beginning to say something queer to me, Tempie, when you came in. It was about Mr. Sevier and I didn't understand. I almost felt that she was being disagreeable to me and it frightened me—about him. I—"

"Law, I spects you is mistook, chile, an' if it war anything she jest wants him herself and was a-laying out ter tell you some enflirtment she had been a-trying ter have with him. Don't pay no 'tention to it." By this time she had regained her composure and was able to reassure Caroline with her usual positiveness to which she added an amount of worldly tact in substituting a highly disturbing thought in place of the dangerous one.

"Do you really think she can be in love with—with him, Tempie?" demanded Caroline Darrah, wide-eyed with astonishment. She was entirely diverted from any desire to follow out or weigh Mrs. Lawrence's remark to her by the wiliness of the experienced Tempie.

"They ain't no telling what widder women out fer number twos *will* do," answered Tempie sagely. "Now, you run and let Miss Annette put that blue frock on you 'fore dinner. In times of disturbance like these here women oughter fix theyselves up so as ter 'tice the men ter eat a little at meal times. Ain't I done put on this white apron ter try and git that no 'count Jefferson jest ter take notice a little uv his vittals. Now go on, honey— it's late."

And thus the love of the old negro had taken away the only chance given Caroline Darrah to learn the facts of the grim story, from the knowledge of which she might have worked out salvation for her lover and herself.

An hour later as they were being served the soup by the absorbed and inattentive Jeff, Mrs. Matilda laid down her spoon and said to Caroline anxiously:

"I wish Phoebe had come out to-night. I asked her but she said she was too busy. She looked tired. Do you suppose she could be ill?"

"Yes," answered the major dryly, "I feel sure that Phoebe is ill. She is at present, I should judge, suffering with a malady which she has had for some time but which is about to reach the acute stage. It needs judicious ignoring so let's not mention it to her for the present."

"I understand what you mean, Major," answered his wife with delighted eyes, "and I won't say a word about it. It will be such a help to David to have a wife when he is the judge. How long will it be before he can be the governor, dear?"

"That depends on the wife, Mrs. Buchanan, to a large extent," answered the major with a delighted smile.

"Oh, Phoebe will want him to do things," said Mrs. Matilda positively.

"No doubt of that," the major replied. "I see David Kildare slated for the full life from now on—eh, Caroline?"

And the major had judged Phoebe's situation perhaps more rightly than he realized, for while David led the vote-directors' rally at the theater and later was closeted with Andrew for hours over the last editorial appeal in the morning *Journal*, Phoebe sat before her desk in her own little down-town home. Mammy Kitty was snoring away like a peaceful watch-dog on her cot in the dressing-room and the whole apartment was dark save for the shaded desk-light.

The time and place were fitting and Phoebe was summoning her visions—and facing her realities. Down the years came sauntering the nonchalant figure of David Kildare. He had asked her to marry him that awful, lonely, sixteenth birthday and he had asked her the same thing every year of all the succeeding ten—and a number of times in between. Phoebe squared herself to her reviewing self and admitted that she had cared for him then and ever since—*cared* for him, but had starved his tenderness and in the lover had left unsought the man. But she was clear-sighted enough to know that the handsome easy-going boy, who had wooed with a smile and taken rebuff with a laugh, was not the steady-eyed forceful man who now faced her. He stood at the door of a life that stretched away into long vistas, and now he would demand. Phoebe bowed her head on her hands—suppose he should not demand!

And so in the watches of the night the siege was raised and Phoebe, the dauntless, brilliant, arrogant Phoebe had capitulated. No love-lorn woman of the ages ever palpitated more thoroughly at the thought of her lover than did she as she kept vigil with David across the city.

But there were articles of capitulation yet to be signed and the ceremony of surrender to come.

CHAPTER XI

ACROSS THE MANY WATERS

And the day of the election arrived next morning and brought cold clouds shot through with occasional gleams of pale sunshine, only to be followed by light but threatening flurries of snow.

All through the Sunday night David had sat over in the editorial rooms of the *Journal* beside Andrew Sevier, talking, writing and sometimes silent with unexpressed sympathy, for as the last sheets of his editorial work slipped through his fingers Andrew grew white and austere. Once for a half-hour they talked about his business affairs and he turned over a bundle of papers to David and discussed the investment of the money that had come from his heavy royalties for the play now running, and the thousands paid in advance for the new drama.

As David ran carefully through them to see that they were in order for him to handle, Andrew turned to his desk and wrote rapidly for some minutes, then sealed a letter and laid it aside. After he had read the last batch of proof from the composing-room he turned to David and with a quiet look handed him the letter which was directed to Caroline Darrah.

"If she ever finds out give her this letter, please. It will make her understand why I go, I hope. I can't talk to you about it but I want to ask you, man to man, to look after her. Dave, I leave her to your care—and Phoebe's." And his rich voice was composed into an utter sadness.

"The work here and the night are both over, let's go down to headquarters," he added, and like two boys, with hands tight gripped, they passed out into the winter street.

Down at the *Gray Picket* they found some of David's ardent supporters still fresh and enthusiastic though they had been making a night of it. Soon waves of excitement were rising and falling all over the city and the streets were thronged with men from out through the county.

At an early hour heavy wagons moved with the measured tread of blind tigers and deposited blind tiger kittens, done up in innocent and deceptive looking crates, at numbers of discreet alley covers near the polls. At the machine headquarters rotund and blooming gentlemen grouped and dissolved and grouped again, during which process wads of greenbacks unrolled and flashed with insolent carelessness. The situation was and had been desperate and this last stand must be brought through for the whisky interest, come high as it would.

And so through the morning, delegations kept dropping in to David's headquarters to keep up the spirits of the candidate and incidentally to have their own raised. There were ugly rumors coming from the polls. The police were machine instruments and the back door of every saloon in the city was wide open, while a repeating vote was plainly indicated by crowds of floaters who drifted from ward to ward. The faces of the bosses were discreetly radiant.

"Lord, David," groaned Cap Cantrell, "they're turning loose kegs of boodle and barrels of booze—we'll never beat 'em in the world! They've got this city tied up and thrown to the dogs! What's the use of—"

"David," exclaimed the major excitedly, "we're in for a rally, and look at them!"

Down the street they came, the news kiddies, a hundred strong, led by Phoebe's freckle-faced red-headed devil whose mouth stretched from ear to ear with a grin. They carried huge poster banners and their inscriptions were in a language of their own, emblazoned in ink-pot script.

"I LOVE MY DAVE—BUT JUMP!" meant much to them but failed to elucidate the fact that they were referring to the gift of a flatboat, canvased for a swimming booth which David had had moored at the foot of the bridge during the dog days of the previous summer so that they might have a joyous dip in the river between editions. He had gone down himself occasionally for a frolic with them and "Jump!" had been the signal for the push-off of any timid diver.

He shouted with glee when he read the skit—he was taking his high dive in life.

"RUN, DAVE, RUN—TIGER'S LOOSE—NIT!" was another witticism and a crooked pole bore aloft these words, "JUDGE DAVID KILDARE SOAKS OLD BOOZE THE FIRST ROUND!"

They lined up in front of the headquarters and gave a shrill cheer that made up in enthusiasm for what it lacked in volume. They took a few words of banter from the candidate in lieu of a speech and paraded off around the city, spending much time in front of the camp of the opposition and indulging in as much of derisive vituperation as they dared.

They were followed by another picturesque visitation. A dignified old colored man brought twenty pathetic little pickaninnies from the orphans' home, to which, the men at headquarters learned for the first time, David Kildare had given the modest building that sheltered the waifs. Decidedly, murder will out, and there come times when the left and right hands of a man are forced into confession to each other about their most secret actions. A political campaign is apt to bring such a situation into the lives of the aspiring candidates. The little coons set up a musical wail that passed for a cheer and marched away munching the contents of a huge box of candy that Polly had sent down to headquarters the night before, such being her idea of a flagon with which to stay the courage of the contestants.

And through it all, the consultation of the leaders, the falling hopes of the poll scouts, the gradual depression that crept over the spirits of the major and Cap and the rest of his near supports, David was a solid tower of strength.

Then during the day the tension became tight and tighter, for how the fight was going exactly no one could tell and it seemed well-nigh impossible to stop the vote steal that was going on all over the city, protected by the organized government. Defeat seemed inevitable.

So at six o'clock the disgusted Cap picked up his hat and started home and to the astonishment of the whole headquarters David Kildare calmly rose and followed him without a word to the others, who failed to realize that he had deserted until he was entirely gone. Billy Bob looked dashed with amazement, Hobson sat down limply in the deserted chair, Tom whistled—but the major looked at them with a quizzical smile which was for a second reflected in Andrew Sevier's face.

Phoebe sat in Milly's little nursery in the failing winter light which was augmented by the glow from the fire of coals.

Little Billy Bob stood at her side within the circle of her arm, his head against her shoulder and his eyes wide with a delicious horror as he gazed upon a calico book whose pages were brilliant with the tragedy of the three bears, which she was reading very slowly and with many explanatory annotations. Crimie balanced himself against her knee and beat with a spoon against the back of the book and whooped up the situation in every bubbly way possible to his lack of classified vocabulary. Milly and Mammy Betty were absorbed in the domestic regions so Phoebe had them all to herself—all four, for the twins lay cuddled asleep in their crib near by.

And though Phoebe had herself well in hand, her mind would wander occasionally from the history of the bruins to which Mistake patiently recalled her by a clamor for, "More, Phoebe, more."

In a hurried response to one of his goads she failed to hear a step in the hall for which she had been telling herself that she had not been listening for two hours or more, and David Kildare stood in the doorway, the firelight full on his face.

It was not a triumphant David with his judiciary honors full upon him and gubernational, senatorial, ambassadorial and presidential astral shapes manifesting themselves in dim perspective; it was just old whimsical David, tender of smile and loving though bantering of eye, albeit a somewhat pale and exhausted edition.

"Phoebe," he said with a low laugh, "nobody wants Dave—for anything!"

And it was then that the fire that had been lighted in the heart of Phoebe in her night watch blazed up into her face as she held out her arms to him! And in the twinkle of a fire-spark David found himself on his knees, with Phoebe, the low chintz-covered chair and the two kiddies clasped to his heart.

For a glorious moment he held them all close and his head rested on Phoebe's shoulder just opposite that of Mistake, while Crimie squirmed between them. Then he discovered that he was gazing under her chin into the wide-open, slightly resentful orbs of Big Brother, who eyed him a moment askance, then, feeling it time to assert himself, reached up and landed a plainly proprietary and challenging kiss against the corner of his lady's mouth.

David laughed delightedly and embraced the trio with greater force as he said propitiatingly, "Good snugglings, isn't it, old man?"

But at this exact moment Crimie took the situation into his own hands, slipped his cable, grabbed the book as he went and rolled over a couple of yards with a delighted giggle. Billy Bob, seeing his treasure captured, instantly followed and there forthwith ensued a tussle that was the height of delight to the two good-natured youngsters.

And Phoebe's arms closed around David more closely as she held him embraced against her shoulder, her soft cheek on his.

"Dave," she whispered, "you know I really don't care at all, don't you?"

"What?" demanded David with alarm in his voice as he raised his head and looked at her in consternation.

"The election makes no—"

"Oh, *that*—I'd forgotten all about it! Don't scare me like that any more, peach-bud, please," he besought and he took her chin in the hollow of his hand as she leant to him, her eyes looking into his, level and confident but glorious with bestowal. For a long minute he gazed straight into their dawn-gray depths then he said gently, the caress suspended:

"Woman, if you are ever going to take any of this back, do it now!"

"Never," she answered and clasped her hands against his breast.

"It's still the loafer out of a job—just Dave-do-nothing," he insisted, a new dignity in his voice that stirred her pride.

"Please!" she closed her eyes as she entreated.

"It's for a long time—*always*." His voice was heaven-sweet with its note of warning and he laid his other strong warm hand on her throat where a controlled sob made it pulse.

"I'm being very patient," she whispered and her lips quivered with a smile as two tears jeweled her black lashes.

But David had made his last stand—he folded her in, locked his heart and threw away the key.

"Love," he whispered after a long time, "I know this is just a dream—I've had 'em for ten years—but don't let anybody wake me!"

To which plea Phoebe was making the tenderest of responses, when the door burst open and Billy Bob shot into the room.

"Hip! hip!" he yelled at the top of his voice, "six hundred and ten plurality and all from the two coon wards—count all in and verified—no difference now how the others go and—" He paused and the situation dawned upon him all in a heap as Phoebe hid her head against David's collar. "Davie," he remarked in subdued tones, "you're 'lected, but I don't s'pose you care!"

"Go away, Billy Bob, don't you see I'm busy?" answered David as he rose to his feet, keeping Phoebe still embraced as she stood beside him.

"Jerusalem the Golden! Have you cornered heaven, David?" gasped Billy Bob again rising to the surface. "Help, somebody, help!" At which exact minute Mistake succeeded in dispossessing Crimie of the last tatters of the adventures of the bears and thus bringing down upon them all a tumult of distraction.

Billy Bob caught up the roarer and threw him almost up to the ceiling. "Hurrah for Dave!" he said, and to the best of his ability Crimie "hurrahed" while Mistake joined in enthusiastically. The hubbub at last penetrated the slumbers of the twins, who added to the uproar to such an extent that Mammy Betty hurried to the scene of action and cleared the deck without further delay.

"And," continued Billy Bob to Milly and the pair of serene and only slightly attentive young people, "you should have seen Jeff, dressed in Dave's last year frock coat and high hat, whizzing around the coon haunts in Caroline's gray car handing out invitations to the Chocolate Country Club jamboree! They put the bottle and the dimes completely out of business and he voted the whole gang straight. They tried hard to fix up the returns but Hob and I were at the count and we saw it clean. Holy smoke, what a sell for the machine! Slipped a cog on the nigger vote that they have handled for years!"

"And not a dollar spent!" said David with pride. Which goes to show that at times women keep their own counsels, for Phoebe ducked her head to hide a smile.

"And now it's up to you to hurry and get to the University Club by eight-thirty. You are to address the populace and two brass bands from the northeast window at nine sharp—two extras out announcing it. Everybody has been looking for you an hour, you old moon-spooner, you!" urged Billy Bob.

"They can keep up the hunt—Phoebe and I are going—well, we are going where nobody can find us for this evening anyway," answered David with danger in his eyes.

"No!" said Phoebe as she slipped her hand into his, "I've had you as long as is fair as it is. Won't you go and see them all? If you will I will dress in a hurry and you can come by for me. Please!"

"Don't pull back on the leash, David," remarked Billy Bob. "It's just beginning. Trot to heel and be happy." He laid his arm round Milly's waist as he spoke and gave her a little squeeze.

And it was into the midst of a glorious round-up of a whole joyous convention of friends that David Kildare stepped several hours later, a resplendent and magnificent David with Phoebe glowing beside him. And, too, it was not only his own high particulars that surged around him, for Phoebe had fixed it with the board of governors and made out a very careful list of every campaign friend he had made and had all the girls at the phones for hours inviting each and every one. If at any time in his political career David Kildare should lack the far vision Phoebe was fully capable of taking a long sight for him.

So Mike O'Rourke was there, stuffed carefully into a rented dress suit and was being attentioned to the point of combustion by Polly, who was thus putting off a reckoning with young New England, promised for "after the election." Freckles, the devil, was having the lark of his life in removing hats and coats under the direction of an extremely dignified club official.

There were men from the down-town district in plain business clothes who stood in excited groups discussing the issues of the day. The head of the cotton mills, who had voted every employee perfectly in line without coercion, was expatiating largely to four old fellows in gray, for whom Cap had succeeded in obtaining furloughs from the commandant out at the Home and was keeping over night as his guests. They also were having the lark of their young lives and were being overwhelmed by attentions from all the Confederate Dames present.

Susie Carrie was wonderful in some dangerously contrived Greek draperies, and over by the window held court on the subject of a city beautiful under a council of artistic city fathers. She announced the beginning of sittings for a full life-sized portrait of Judge Kildare for the city hall, at which Billy Bob raised such a cheer as almost to drown out the orchestra.

Mrs. Buchanan received everybody with the most beaming delight and Mrs. Shelby was so excited that she asked Billy

Bob about the children, which concession brought the stars to Milly's gentle eyes.

Mrs. Cherry, as usual, was in full and resplendent regalia with Tom in attendance, displaying a satisfied and masterful manner that told its own tale. Her amazing encounter with Tempie had remained a secret between her and the discreet old negro and her manner to Caroline Darrah was so impressively cordial that Phoebe actually unbent to the extent of an exchange of congratulations that had a semblance of friendliness. The widow's net having hauled up Tom, hopes for untroubled waters again could be indulged.

In the midst of all the hilarity the delegations and the bands began to arrive outside. The cheering rose to a roar and from the brilliantly lighted ballroom David Kildare stepped out on the balcony and stood forty-five minutes laughing and bowing, not managing to get in more than a few words of what might have been a great speech if his constituency had not been entirely too excited to listen to it.

It was almost midnight when they all marched away to *Dixie* played to rag-time measure and sung by five hundred strong. With a sigh of relief David held out his arms to Phoebe and started to swing her into the whirl of the dancers. As his arms fell about her Phoebe pressed close to him with a quick breath and his eyes followed hers across the room.

Under the lights that hung above the entrance to the fern room stood Caroline Darrah like a flower blown against the deep green of the tall palms behind her, and her eyes were lifted to Andrew's face which smiled down at her with suppressed tragedy. For an instant she laid her hand on his arm and they were about to catch step with the music when suddenly she swung around into the green tangle beyond her and reached out her hand to draw him after her.

"Pray, David, pray," said Phoebe as they glided over the polished floor.

"I am," David whispered back as his arms tightened. "I can't think of anything but 'Now I lay me'—but won't it help?"

In the wide window at the end of the long room Caroline turned and waited for Andrew. The lights from the city beat up into her face and she was pale, while her jewel eyes shone black under their long lashes. Her white gloved hands wrung themselves against his breast as she held him from her.

"Out there while we danced," she whispered, "I don't know what, but something told me that you are going to leave me and not tell me why. You were saying good-by to my heart— with yours. Tell me, what is it?"

And with full knowledge of the strange, subtle, superconscious thing that had been between them from the first and which had manifested itself in devious mystic ways, Andrew Sevier had dared to think he could hold her in his arms in an atmosphere charged with the call of a half-barbarous music and take farewell of her—she all unknowing of what threatened!

"What is it?" she demanded again and her hands separated to clasp his shoulder convulsively. Her words were a flutter between her teeth.

Then the God of Women struck light across his blindness, and taking her in his arms, he looked her straight in the eyes and told her the whole gruesome bitter tale. Before he had finished she closed her eyes against his and swayed away from him to the cold window-pane.

"I see," she whispered, "you don't want me—you couldn't— *you—never—did*!"

And at that instant the blood bond in Andrew Sevier's breast snapped and with an awed comprehension of the vast and everlasting Source from which flows the love that constrains and the love that heals, the love that only comes to bind in honor, he reached out and took his own. In the seventh heaven which is the soul haunt of all in like case, there was no need of word mating.

Hours later, one by one the lights in the houses along the avenue twinkled out and the street lay in the grasp of the after midnight silence. Only a bright light still burned at the major's table, which was piled high with books into which he was delving with the hunger of many long hours of deprivation strong upon him. He had scouted the idea of the ball, had donned dressing-gown and slippers and gone back to the company of his Immortals with alacrity. On their return Mrs. Buchanan and the girls had found him buried in his tomes ten deep and it was with difficulty that Phoebe, kneeling beside him on one side, and Caroline on the other, made him listen to their joint tale of modern romance, to which Mrs. Matilda played the part of a joyous commentator.

To Phoebe he was merciless and a war of wits made the library echo with its give and take.

"Of course, my dear Phoebe," he said, "it is an established fact that a man and his wife are one, and if you will just let that one be Judge Kildare semi-occasionally it will more than content him, I'm sure."

"Why, Major, can't you trust me to be a good—wife to David? Don't be unkind to me! I'll promise to—to—"

"Don't, Phoebe, don't! That 'love, honor and obey' clause is the direct cause of all the woman legislation ever undertaken—and it holds a remarkably short time after marriage as a general thing. Now there's Matilda—for over thirty-five years I've—But where is Andrew?" he demanded anxiously.

"Andy," answered David with the greatest delight in his happy eyes and the red lock rampant over his brow, "is sitting on the end of a hard bench down at the telegraph office trying to get a cable through to his chief for permission to wait over for a steamer that sails for Panama two weeks from to-day."

"What?" demanded the major in surprise, looking at Caroline.

"Oh, *she's* going with him—there are no frills to the affection of Caroline Darrah! She'll be bending over his camp-fire yanking out his hot tamales in less than a month—glad to do it. Won't you, beautiful?" answered David gleefully to Caroline's beautiful confusion.

"David Kildare," observed the major with the utmost solemnity, "when a man and woman embark with love at the rudder it is well the Almighty controls the wind and the tides."

"I know, Major, I know and I'm scared some, only I'm counting on Phoebe's chart and the stars. I'm just the jolly paddler," answered David with a laugh across at Phoebe.

"Well," remarked the major judicially, "I think she will be able to accomplish the course if undisturbed. It will behoove you, however, to remember that husband love is a steady combustion, not a conflagration."

"What do you call a love that has burned constantly for between ten and fifteen years, Major?" asked David as he smiled into the keen old eyes that held his.

"That," answered the major, "is a fire fit to light an altar, sir."

"And in my heart, ah, Major, can you trust me—to keep—it burning?" said Phoebe, thus making her avowal before them all with gallant voice and eyes of the dawn.

Moments later after Phoebe and Mrs. Buchanan had retired down the hall, and up the stairway, Caroline Darrah still knelt by the major's chair. They were both silent and the major held her hand in his. They neither of them heard the latch key and in a moment Andrew Sevier stood across the firelight from them.

"I wanted to hear it, Major," he entreated as he laid his hand on Caroline's shoulder when she came to his side and held out his other to the major. "Say it, if you will, sir!"

"The Almighty bless you, boy, and make His sun to shine upon you. He is doing it in giving you Caroline to wife. Some women He holds as hostages until the greater men in us can rise to claim them and to-night His eyes have seen your fulfilment." The major looked straight into the pain-ravaged but radiant face before him and his keen old eyes glowed through the mist that spread across them.

"Child," he said after a moment's silence as he laid his hand on Caroline's other shoulder, "across the many waters that can not drown love you have brought back to my old age young Andrew the Glad."

Choose from Thousands of 1stWorldLibrary Classics By

A. M. Barnard
Ada Leverson
Adolphus William Ward
Aesop
Agatha Christie
Alexander Aaronsohn
Alexander Kielland
Alexandre Dumas
Alfred Gatty
Alfred Ollivant
Alice Duer Miller
Alice Turner Curtis
Alice Dunbar
Allen Chapman
Alleyne Ireland
Ambrose Bierce
Amelia E. Barr
Amory H. Bradford
Andrew Lang
Andrew McFarland Davis
Andy Adams
Angela Brazil
Anna Alice Chapin
Anna Sewell
Annie Besant
Annie Hamilton Donnell
Annie Payson Call
Annie Roe Carr
Annonaymous
Anton Chekhov
Archibald Lee Fletcher
Arnold Bennett
Arthur C. Benson
Arthur Conan Doyle
Arthur M. Winfield
Arthur Ransome
Arthur Schnitzler
Arthur Train
Atticus
B.H. Baden-Powell
B. M. Bower
B. C. Chatterjee
Baroness Emmuska Orczy
Baroness Orczy
Basil King
Bayard Taylor
Ben Macomber
Bertha Muzzy Bower
Bjornstjerne Bjornson

Booth Tarkington
Boyd Cable
Bram Stoker
C. Collodi
C. E. Orr
C. M. Ingleby
Carolyn Wells
Catherine Parr Traill
Charles A. Eastman
Charles Amory Beach
Charles Dickens
Charles Dudley Warner
Charles Farrar Browne
Charles Ives
Charles Kingsley
Charles Klein
Charles Hanson Towne
Charles Lathrop Pack
Charles Romyn Dake
Charles Whibley
Charles Willing Beale
Charlotte M. Braeme
Charlotte M. Yonge
Charlotte Perkins Stetson
Clair W. Hayes
Clarence Day Jr.
Clarence E. Mulford
Clemence Housman
Confucius
Coningsby Dawson
Cornelis DeWitt Wilcox
Cyril Burleigh
D. H. Lawrence
Daniel Defoe
David Garnett
Dinah Craik
Don Carlos Janes
Donald Keyhoe
Dorothy Kilner
Dougan Clark
Douglas Fairbanks
E. Nesbit
E. P. Roe
E. Phillips Oppenheim
E. S. Brooks
Earl Barnes
Edgar Rice Burroughs
Edith Van Dyne
Edith Wharton

Edward Everett Hale
Edward J. O'Biren
Edward S. Ellis
Edwin L. Arnold
Eleanor Atkins
Eleanor Hallowell Abbott
Eliot Gregory
Elizabeth Gaskell
Elizabeth McCracken
Elizabeth Von Arnim
Ellem Key
Emerson Hough
Emilie F. Carlen
Emily Bronte
Emily Dickinson
Enid Bagnold
Enilor Macartney Lane
Erasmus W. Jones
Ernie Howard Pie
Ethel May Dell
Ethel Turner
Ethel Watts Mumford
Eugene Sue
Eugenie Foa
Eugene Wood
Eustace Hale Ball
Evelyn Everett-green
Everard Cotes
F. H. Cheley
F. J. Cross
F. Marion Crawford
Fannie E. Newberry
Federick Austin Ogg
Ferdinand Ossendowski
Fergus Hume
Florence A. Kilpatrick
Fremont B. Deering
Francis Bacon
Francis Darwin
Frances Hodgson Burnett
Frances Parkinson Keyes
Frank Gee Patchin
Frank Harris
Frank Jewett Mather
Frank L. Packard
Frank V. Webster
Frederic Stewart Isham
Frederick Trevor Hill
Frederick Winslow Taylor

Friedrich Kerst
Friedrich Nietzsche
Fyodor Dostoyevsky
G.A. Henty
G.K. Chesterton
Gabrielle E. Jackson
Garrett P. Serviss
Gaston Leroux
George A. Warren
George Ade
Geroge Bernard Shaw
George Cary Eggleston
George Durston
George Ebers
George Eliot
George Gissing
George MacDonald
George Meredith
George Orwell
George Sylvester Viereck
George Tucker
George W. Cable
George Wharton James
Gertrude Atherton
Gordon Casserly
Grace E. King
Grace Gallatin
Grace Greenwood
Grant Allen
Guillermo A. Sherwell
Gulielma Zollinger
Gustav Flaubert
H. A. Cody
H. B. Irving
H.C. Bailey
H. G. Wells
H. H. Munro
H. Irving Hancock
H. R. Naylor
H. Rider Haggard
H. W. C. Davis
Haldeman Julius
Hall Caine
Hamilton Wright Mabie
Hans Christian Andersen
Harold Avery
Harold McGrath
Harriet Beecher Stowe
Harry Castlemon
Harry Coghill
Harry Houidini

Hayden Carruth
Helent Hunt Jackson
Helen Nicolay
Hendrik Conscience
Hendy David Thoreau
Henri Barbusse
Henrik Ibsen
Henry Adams
Henry Ford
Henry Frost
Henry James
Henry Jones Ford
Henry Seton Merriman
Henry W Longfellow
Herbert A. Giles
Herbert Carter
Herbert N. Casson
Herman Hesse
Hildegard G. Frey
Homer
Honore De Balzac
Horace B. Day
Horace Walpole
Horatio Alger Jr.
Howard Pyle
Howard R. Garis
Hugh Lofting
Hugh Walpole
Humphry Ward
Ian Maclaren
Inez Haynes Gillmore
Irving Bacheller
Isabel Cecilia Williams
Isabel Hornibrook
Israel Abrahams
Ivan Turgenev
J.G.Austin
J. Henri Fabre
J. M. Barrie
J. M. Walsh
J. Macdonald Oxley
J. R. Miller
J. S. Fletcher
J. S. Knowles
J. Storer Clouston
J. W. Duffield
Jack London
Jacob Abbott
James Allen
James Andrews
James Baldwin

James Branch Cabell
James DeMille
James Joyce
James Lane Allen
James Lane Allen
James Oliver Curwood
James Oppenheim
James Otis
James R. Driscoll
Jane Abbott
Jane Austen
Jane L. Stewart
Janet Aldridge
Jens Peter Jacobsen
Jerome K. Jerome
Jessie Graham Flower
John Buchan
John Burroughs
John Cournos
John F. Kennedy
John Gay
John Glasworthy
John Habberton
John Joy Bell
John Kendrick Bangs
John Milton
John Philip Sousa
John Taintor Foote
Jonas Lauritz Idemil Lie
Jonathan Swift
Joseph A. Altsheler
Joseph Carey
Joseph Conrad
Joseph E. Badger Jr
Joseph Hergesheimer
Joseph Jacobs
Jules Vernes
Julian Hawthrone
Julie A Lippmann
Justin Huntly McCarthy
Kakuzo Okakura
Karle Wilson Baker
Kate Chopin
Kenneth Grahame
Kenneth McGaffey
Kate Langley Bosher
Kate Langley Bosher
Katherine Cecil Thurston
Katherine Stokes
L. A. Abbot
L. T. Meade

L. Frank Baum	Paul G. Tomlinson	T. S. Arthur
Latta Griswold	Paul Severing	The Princess Der Ling
Laura Dent Crane	Percy Brebner	Thomas A. Janvier
Laura Lee Hope	Percy Keese Fitzhugh	Thomas A Kempis
Laurence Housman	Peter B. Kyne	Thomas Anderton
Lawrence Beasley	Plato	Thomas Bailey Aldrich
Leo Tolstoy	Quincy Allen	Thomas Bulfinch
Leonid Andreyev	R. Derby Holmes	Thomas De Quincey
Lewis Carroll	R. L. Stevenson	Thomas Dixon
Lewis Sperry Chafer	R. S. Ball	Thomas H. Huxley
Lilian Bell	Rabindranath Tagore	Thomas Hardy
Lloyd Osbourne	Rahul Alvares	Thomas More
Louis Hughes	Ralph Bonehill	Thornton W. Burgess
Louis Joseph Vance	Ralph Henry Barbour	U. S. Grant
Louis Tracy	Ralph Victor	Upton Sinclair
Louisa May Alcott	Ralph Waldo Emmerson	Valentine Williams
Lucy Fitch Perkins	Rene Descartes	Various Authors
Lucy Maud Montgomery	Ray Cummings	Vaughan Kester
Luther Benson	Rex Beach	Victor Appleton
Lydia Miller Middleton	Rex E. Beach	Victor G. Durham
Lyndon Orr	Richard Harding Davis	Victoria Cross
M. Corvus	Richard Jefferies	Virginia Woolf
M. H. Adams	Richard Le Gallienne	Wadsworth Camp
Margaret E. Sangster	Robert Barr	Walter Camp
Margret Howth	Robert Frost	Walter Scott
Margaret Vandercook	Robert Gordon Anderson	Washington Irving
Margaret W. Hungerford	Robert L. Drake	Wilbur Lawton
Margret Penrose	Robert Lansing	Wilkie Collins
Maria Edgeworth	Robert Lynd	Willa Cather
Maria Thompson Daviess	Robert Michael Ballantyne	Willard F. Baker
Mariano Azuela	Robert W. Chambers	William Dean Howells
Marion Polk Angellotti	Rosa Nouchette Carey	William le Queux
Mark Overton	Rudyard Kipling	W. Makepeace Thackeray
Mark Twain	Saint Augustine	William W. Walter
Mary Austin	Samuel B. Allison	William Shakespeare
Mary Catherine Crowley	Samuel Hopkins Adams	Winston Churchill
Mary Cole	Sarah Bernhardt	Yei Theodora Ozaki
Mary Hastings Bradley	Sarah C. Hallowell	Yogi Ramacharaka
Mary Roberts Rinehart	Selma Lagerlof	Young E. Allison
Mary Rowlandson	Sherwood Anderson	Zane Grey
M. Wollstonecraft Shelley	Sigmund Freud	
Maud Lindsay	Standish O'Grady	
Max Beerbohm	Stanley Weyman	
Myra Kelly	Stella Benson	
Nathaniel Hawthrone	Stella M. Francis	
Nicolo Machiavelli	Stephen Crane	
O. F. Walton	Stewart Edward White	
Oscar Wilde	Stijn Streuvels	
Owen Johnson	Swami Abhedananda	
P.G. Wodehouse	Swami Parmananda	
Paul and Mabel Thorne	T. S. Ackland